"With short, propulsive chapters, Sara Mesa creates an un-forgettable gothic landscape, centered on the mysterious and menacing Wybrany College, that twists in ways that unsettle and thrill. In *Four by Four*, Mesa's sentences are clear as glass, but when you look through you will be terrified by what you see."
—**Laura van den Berg**

"The atmospheric unraveling of the mystery will keep you turning the page; the ending will leave you stunned—Mesa's *Four by Four* is a tautly written literary thriller that juxtaposes the innocence of children with the fetish of control; a social parable that warns against the silence of oppression and isolation through its disquieting, sparse prose."
—**Kelsey Westenberg, Seminary Co-op**

"Stylistically, *Four by Four*'s narrative structure is both dazzling and dizzying, as its perfect pacing only enhances the metastasizing dread and dis-ease. . . . Mesa exposes the thin veneer of venerability to be hiding something menacing and unforgivable—and *Four by Four* lays it bare for all the world to see."
—**Jeremy Garber, Powell's Books**

"What can I say about a story in which everything works? . . . A new author that will surprise us further in future."
—**Sergio Sancor, *Libros y literatura***

# Bad Handwriting

## Sara Mesa

### TRANSLATED BY KATIE WHITTEMORE

*Curated by Katie Whittemore for the 2022 Translator Triptych*

OPEN LETTER
LITERARY TRANSLATIONS FROM THE UNIVERSITY OF ROCHESTER

Originally published in Spanish as *Mala letra* by Anagrama

Copyright © 2016 by Sara Mesa

Translation copyright © 2022 by Katie Whittemore

First Open Letter edition, 2022

Library of Congress Cataloging-in-Publication Data: Available.

ISBN-13: 9781948830553

Ebook ISBN: 9781948830737

*This project is supported in part by an award from the National Endowment for the Arts and the New York State Council on the Arts with the support of the Governor of New York State and the New York State Legislature.*

*Support for the translation of this book was provided by Acción Cultural Española, AC/E*

**AC/E**
ACCIÓN CULTURAL
ESPAÑOLA

Printed on acid-free paper in the United States of America

Cover Design by Anna Morrison

Interior Design by Anuj Mathur

Open Letter is the University of Rochester's nonprofit, literary translation press: Dewey Hall 1-219, Box 278968, Rochester NY 14627

www.openletterbooks.org

# CONTENTS

# THE SCREECH OWL

FROM THE TOP OF THE HILL the girl turned and saw the others around the picnic table. The conversation was an unintelligible murmur off in the distance, like the buzzing of bees. The sun was setting and the light was vanishing from the pines, revealing deep greens and hollows that had remained hidden during the day. She breathed in the air—damp earth, lavender and rosemary, cow shit flattened by a car tire—and returned to the others, lagging. The snap of the pine needles breaking beneath her feet grew quieter as she drew near, strangled by the voice of the aunt, a voice from the depths of an earthen jar, deep, strong, stony. The others were gathered around her, finishing up the last bits of supper, seeking her permission, waiting their turn with restrained scrupulousness. The aunt always knew exactly what had to be done and the proper steps to do it. She had slowly dished out the butter, the foie gras, the slices of toasted bread, the coffee, allowing no one to disturb her ritual. She performed it deliberately, unhurried, as if time itself was obliged to mold to her pace. Her words filled the esplanade and extended beyond the

1

smooth boggy hills. The girl stopped to watch her from a few yards away. It was her twenty-second birthday and this was the entirety of the celebration they granted her: pine forest, cars, supper in the countryside, a family gathering with old friends that weren't even hers.

In one of the cars off to the side, her uncle was clipping his toenails, his skinny legs hanging out the door. There was an almost religious concentration in the rigid set of his jaw.

"Time to start picking up," he said when he'd finished, looking at the horizon. "It's getting dark."

He tucked the clippers in his shirt pocket and turned his baggy eyes to the table. The aunt went on talking as if she hadn't heard. Her speech—clipped, abrupt—did not allow for interruptions. She had extremely fine wrinkles above her lip. From a distance, they gave the impression of a very sparse but soldierly mustache.

"These days everyone talks about solidarity and commitment. There are thousands of campaigns and protests and petitions for one cause or another. But you have to take care of your own first, isn't that right? Helping people from far away, bah, that's easy. Give to charity? Send old clothes to Africa? Sponsor a kid? There's no merit in any of it. What *is* hard is being there, every second, for your own people. Looking out for them, not letting them down, teaching them to carry on, not letting them get lost or off track. Now that's really *doing something*, the rest doesn't count."

The couple sitting next to her—a thick and bosomy redhead and her husband, small and reserved—nodded as they chewed. They'd been the aunt and uncle's neighbors for many years and were familiar with her ways. They kept their mouths shut and showed their agreement with slight movements of their heads. A boy about six years old sat a little way away. He was dark-haired, freckled, lost in thought, an absorbed look on his impassive face. He ate his toasted baguette indifferently, throwing away the burnt edges of the bread. The redhead admonished him with a wink, but the aunt caught on immediately.

"Oh come on! Eat nicely, would you? You'll be skin and bones if you carry on like that! Don't play with your food!"

She changed her tone and turned to the redhead, narrowing her eyes. She emphasized certain words, as if the mere uttering of them disgusted her.

"If it were up to him, he'd eat nothing but *junk*. Parents these days don't make any effort. A nice piece of toast for an afternoon snack? Oh no, that's *old-fashioned!* A donut or slice of pizza is *so* much better. His mother pays no attention to him. Typical of that part of the family—must be genetic. Women having babies young and then *abandoning* them. We raised this one, too," she added, nodding toward the boy.

The boy watched his mother closely as she continued to make her way down the hill, staring at the toes of her shoes. The girl looked up and smiled at him weakly. He stood up, his growing body skinny and awkward, and with the toast still in hand approached the uncle, who was putting out the last embers of the campfire. A few coals still burned among the charred logs. The man threw fistfuls of earth on them, taking care not to dirty himself. A magpie flew overhead, the sound of its caw suspended in the air.

"Silvio's not here," the boy announced.

The aunt looked at him. Her eyes blazed. The boy flushed. His freckles stood out even more against his skin.

"Where is he?" she shrieked.

Nobody knew how to respond. They'd already folded the table, loaded the cars, put the trash in bags. The uncle closed the trunk of his Fiat and rubbed his hands together. They'd have to take a look around, he said looking at the sky. Pink and mauve clouds broke apart, admitting the last rays of light. An inhospitable dampness rose from the ground.

"*A look around?* Doesn't he know what time it is? What's that nephew of yours thinking?"

The redhead tried to calm her. He must have gotten distracted, that's all. Silvio knew the countryside well, her husband observed from off to the side, stepping on the smoking remnants of the fire. He wasn't a kid anymore, he wasn't going to get lost.

"I know he's not going to get lost! But we can't wait around for him forever! We have to go!"

The boy looked around and in a soft voice suggested that they call his mobile. *Call his mobile!* brayed the aunt. Everyone knew they didn't have service there. The neighbors looked at her for a moment, unsettled, not knowing what to do. The uncle opened the trunk again and busied himself rearranging the bags. The aunt threw a shawl over her shoulders, as if all the cold in the air had suddenly descended on her alone, wrinkled her brow and continued to mutter without taking her eyes off the path.

"I'll go look for him," the girl told her aunt. "I'll take the boy."

She didn't wait for permission. She took the boy by the hand and started off toward the hill, leaving the two older couples behind in the mist of the growing dusk. The screeching of the magpies cut across the sky. She tried to match her steps to those of her son.

They called for him several times, first in one direction, then the other. There was no response from Silvio. The girl grabbed the boy by the arm and forced him to walk faster. They would probably find him next to the creek, or what little was left of the creek: a broken stream of chocolate-colored, stinking water, bordered by cattails and yellowing reeds, the slippery and swampy land pockmarked with rabbit burrows and poisonous mushrooms, their stems bent by disease. The girl remembered that as children they had caught frogs there, armed with a colander. As the eldest, she'd been the one to go into the water—cold, biting, green—taking care not to splash too much, while Silvio waited, crouched on the bank, keeping quiet with absolute seriousness. Once they'd trapped the frogs, they put them in glass jars filled with water and examined them closely. The frogs almost always ended up suffocating to death, they didn't really know why. The image of a frog floating in the water, its thick legs limp, was one of indescribable sadness. The girl shook off the memory. After all, she thought, there hadn't been frogs there in a long time.

The boy shouted, his throat tight: it was a sharp, child-like call, tinged with uncertainty. There was no answer.

"It's getting dark, mamá" he whispered. "Let's go back. Tito Silvio isn't out here."

The girl stopped to think. They could cross the creek by jumping on some stones without too much risk of getting wet. On the other side, the forest stretched out darkly, impenetrable, rustling with pine needles and the fallen bud scales of eucalyptus trees. Or they could stay on this side, and continue the search by following the stream until reaching the little dirt road they'd passed that morning upon arriving, the cars still clean and full of food.

"Come," she said. "We're going to cross the creek."

The boy looked behind him fearfully. The purring of a whip-poor-will, the darkness rushing toward him. He swallowed and, grabbing onto the girl, clambered down the slope. They moved forward slowly, holding hands, their shoes sinking in the mud, until they reached the edge of the water. The stream was almost nonexistent; the middle of the creek couldn't have been more than a foot and a half deep. They could hardly make out the stones, flat and muddied, in the shadows. The girl tried to calm the boy. Just step really carefully, she told him, put his feet exactly where she put hers. Silvio would be on the other side, she was certain.

The creek stunk of stagnant water and rot. The boy whimpered but the girl squeezed his hand and made her way from stone to stone. They went slowly and silently, so as not to lose their concentration. When they stopped talking, the forest filled with sounds: the rustling of reeds, the cry of a small owl, an animal—a rabbit, a rat—running through the rushes, the impossibly far-off rumble of a car.

"Silvio!" yelled the boy, desperate. Then he slipped, falling into the water.

She didn't have anything to clean him with. The girl used her own T-shirt to wipe the mud off his legs. His sneakers were dripping; she dried them as best she could and he put them back on. The boy reeked of dirty water. She consoled him for several minutes, humming and cooing. When they stood up, night had fallen completely.

"Mamá, shouldn't we go back?"

The boy peered into the darkness of the forest, his pupils dilated. Disheveled locks of hair fell over his ears. His profile blurred into the blackness.

"Don't worry. We're going the right way. I'm sure we'll find Silvio out here."

They called out several more times, feeling their way through the shadows of the trees. Cold and shining silhouettes could still be made out, bathed in moonlight and the glow from some nearby town. The boy moved even closer to the girl and they continued for a few yards, until they couldn't go any further. They stayed silent and still, their feet on a cushioned and invisible blanket of leaves.

The question was whether they should try to go back. Crossing the creek again was not an option. By now the forest was a *camera obscura*, where all identity—of a tree, a thicket, a stone, a puddle—was entirely dissolved. Small insects landed on their exposed calves. All around them were the sounds of leaves and branches creaking swiftly, nocturnal rodents seeking new hiding places as they fled the barn owls. The reedy, tremulous, drawn-out shriek of a screech owl sounded from a distance, then drew near with a short, chaotic flapping of wings.

*Hoo-hoo-hoo-hoo-hoo.*

"It wants us to leave," the boy whispered.

The girl didn't answer. The owl circled overhead for several minutes. Eventually, they felt it land somewhere close by.

"Are we lost?" the boy sobbed, clutching at the girl's arm.

"We're fine!" the girl shouted, suddenly irritable. "Stop whining! You're with your mother, you hear me? *You're with your mother!* Nothing is going to happen to you! We're not in the middle of the jungle! We're just in some shitty woods by a shitty creek by a bunch of shitty towns and shitty roads! That's all!"

The boy broke into tears and the girl gathered him up in her arms.


Advancing a few more yards, they shouted as loudly as they could, standing on their tiptoes. At times they stopped to rest and listen for someone, in the distance, calling for them. The only sound was the ominous *hoo-hoo-hoo-hoo* of the screech owl as it glided overhead.

"It wants us to leave," the boy repeated.

"Don't worry. We'll go sooner or later. Are you cold?"

"No, but I'm really tired."

"Okay, now listen to me. We're going to lie down to rest a bit and wait until morning. It's okay. This is an adventure, right?"

"Lie down where?"

"Come here," she said.

They went to the foot of a tree and leaned against its trunk. Then the girl crouched down and patted the ground with both hands. It was too hard, with small pointy sticks poking up through ground and scratchy plants, some kind of fern, sprouting wildly here and there. They looked for another tree nearby, feeling their way, stepping slowly, close together with their arms stretched out in the emptiness before them. The screech owl passed overhead again, almost brushing them. The girl cleared the sticks from another patch of earth. The boy stood at her side, controlling his sobs. The girl whispered to him as if he were a baby. *Shhh, easy, child.* Some kind of spider or caterpillar crawled across her hand, but she shook it off and repressed a scream. She smoothed the leaves as best she could, breathing heavily. Afterward, she took off her sweatshirt and spread it on the ground, fluffing up the hood near the base of the tree.

"Come here," she told him.

She guided the boy to the sweatshirt and showed him where to lie down. Then she stretched out beside him and wrapped him in her arms. The screech owl perched in the tree under which they lay.

*The scent he gives off is sharply sweet and innocent. The boy fell right to sleep, exhausted, and now she can feel his deep and uneasy breathing, interrupted at times by the gust of fear that shakes him. She squeezes his body to give him every molecule of warmth, every single molecule of warmth that can possibly be transmitted by her touch. Curled up at his back, wrapping her woman's legs around his childish ones, she gently breathes in the smell of his defenseless little neck, thinking how he was still only half-grown. Despite the sounds, the creaks, the distant cries, despite even the penetrating call of the screech owl, she can hear the uneven beating of his pulse, ripping open the night. He's my son, she tells herself, he's my son.*

Two hours or so had passed when the girl heard voices and the barking of dogs. She opened her eyes and made out beams of light that disappeared, then swung back toward them, the flashing of dreams. As the barking drew closer, the owl flew off, hooting and beating its wings. The girl hugged the boy and remained still a little longer, holding her breath, drinking in the last moment of freedom, until the boy turned and abruptly sat up, frightened.

"What's happening, mamá? Who's there?"

"Nothing," she whispered slowly. "It's okay, they've found us."

They got up and before they could see them, they felt the dogs panting, running to the approaching shadows and returning again to touch their hands with slobbering muzzles. A flashlight shone full in their faces. Her forearm covering her eyes, the girl pulled the boy in close.

"We're here," she said.

"Oh, thank God."

The figure of Silvio stood out against the darkness; a huge, warm body standing over them, shouting for a blanket. The boy began to cry again. The girl felt like she was wrapped in a dense and murky confusion. *The sins of the past,* she remembered. Those words. She felt dizzy. Heart racing, still not moving, she heard the others, their shouts, their noise; the crisscrossing beams of light, the euphoric barking of the dogs as they circled, the questions, the sighs, the smooth touch of the boy's hand, the unmistakable beeping of the walkie-talkies, the deep voices of the officers giving instructions that she couldn't quite manage to understand.

Someone came up from behind and roughly grabbed her arm.

"Let's go, girl, get moving, we have to get you back. What ever possessed you to go into the woods with a child this time of night? Bundle him up and follow us. Your family's waiting."

Without letting go of the boy, scarcely giving an answer, she staggered after them, dragging her feet. Through the barking of the dogs, she listened for the cry of the owl. She heard nothing.

# MÁRMOL

WE HAD VERY LIMITED experience with death in those days. Occasionally, someone's grandfather or grandmother would die, like a domino whose turn it is to fall, but almost all of us had at least two or three living grandparents. Some grandparents—grandmothers, mostly—jumped off the balcony. This happened with some frequency back then; I've since wondered if it was something particular to that neighborhood or time, a coincidence or distortion of my memory. Whatever the case may be, it did happen, or at least I remember it happening. We were just playing in the street when first we heard the rumors, then the shouting: so-and-so's grandmother had jumped from the fourth story, the fifth story, the tenth story, always high enough to kill herself. The apartment blocks—subsidized housing of exposed brick—were tall, with narrow balconies crammed with junk. Cleaning supplies, birdcages without birds, plastic planters without plants, even old, dirty mattresses. Some balconies had been enclosed with frosted glass, but even this, it appeared, didn't stop the old ladies from climbing up and jumping to their deaths. It was like a plague.

Five or six jumped in the span of a couple of years. Once we even saw the body—from a distance and behind the police tape and huddled neighbors—smashed on the sidewalk, limp as a rag. Only our fear held us back, and maybe disgust. And nothing stopped us from inventing, perversely, the possibility of a murder. I bet she was pushed, someone said, they did it for the inheritance, another kid would add. We repeated plots from made-for-TV movies, even though in our neighborhood the grandmothers didn't leave any inheritance, and never had.

Grandparents died, but for us, life was limitless. After all, what can a child understand about death? Or rather, what can a child understand about death in a country free of war and conflict, in a medium-sized city in a moderately developed country, in a normal neighborhood like so many other indistinguishable and interchangeable neighborhoods, the expansive working-class outskirts, with their straight streets and little plazas where we spent the afternoons in boredom— the ball, the jump rope, the flirting, and the lies—with those tall brick apartment buildings where widowed grandmothers were taken in by their families—and tucked away in a corner, perhaps—grandmothers who every so often, conscientiously and methodically, died of old age or maybe, tired of waiting, threw themselves out the window.

We had other concerns, like for instance: how to get the most sought-after stamp to complete a collection—not because you had an actual collection to complete, but to make yourself seem important in front of the other kids—or how to avoid being teased for wearing good-girl shoes to school instead of sneakers. Or how to pretend that you were allowed to watch the show that everybody else watched except you, or how to get good grades without being labeled a kiss-ass, how to draw caricatures of all the teachers—I was good at that—without getting caught and made to stand facing the wall, and how to avoid getting scolded for holding your pencil wrong, how to avoid being forced to hold it correctly and falling behind during dictation.

Sometimes, too, there were other worries that pulsed with an unhealthy satisfaction, something like the thrill of sensing a torn and vulnerable interior, of peering into an abyss, unable to clearly distinguish the shapes below. Those were the days of the phone calls, the unsettling—and seductive—days of the phone calls. Every afternoon, right when my mother brought my brother to his music lessons, somebody called the house and I was the one who picked up. Day after day, a distorted but unmistakably adult voice on the other end of the line rolled out the same threat with astonishing languor: "Your father is going to die. We're going to kill him." Just that, over and over, the warning in its measured, malicious cadence: "Your father is going to die. We're going to kill him. Your father is going to die. We're going to kill him." The receiver pressed to my ear, frozen in fear, I did nothing. I didn't respond, I didn't ask questions, I barely breathed: I simply listened until I couldn't take any more, then hung up. My mother went out every afternoon, Monday through Friday, and I sat and waited for the phone call that never failed to come and must have been perfectly planned because they never called on the weekends. I was terrified—I started to think that they really would kill my father—but I never dared say anything to anyone. In part,

I was held back by a strange superstition that somehow it would end up happening if I talked. But there was also the desire to hoard the panic for myself, the immense, unadulterated suffering that ringed me in the middle of the night, unshared, my own.

During the day at school, I would keep hearing that voice inside my head. I was thinking of it with a shudder—*Your father is going to die. We're going to kill him*—when one of the ubiquitous Rubio penmanship books was brought down on my desk, louder, more violent than one would expect from paper on wood.

"Can you not write properly, the way God intended? Look at this!"

It was the science teacher again, obsessed with how I held my pencil. Your hand looks like a stump, he'd say, you're going to get calluses on your fingers, your handwriting is atrocious when you hold it like that, you're going to write properly, whatever it takes. Properly! Whatever it takes! he would repeat, showing me the back cover of the notebook with the little drawings of two hands—is this clear enough for you?—one holding the pencil *right*, and one holding it *wrong*. *The secret to harmonious and delicate handwriting is to hold the pen correctly, lightly, and always write slowly,* (not like me, rough, pig-headed, stubborn as a mule), you insist on doing it wrong on purpose. I'd swallow, hold back my tears, and try to position my fingers the I was supposed to—the way God, apparently, had intended—the index finger poised lightly atop the pencil, the thumb below, supporting it, not bending, not pressing down, now come on, write, faster, come on, write.

15

But I wrote slowly that way, and I always fell behind when he gave us dictations. You don't ever learn and you don't want to learn, he'd shout at me, you're going to end up illiterate. How I would love to tell that teacher now—if he's still alive, that is—that despite holding my pencil the wrong way, despite my bad handwriting, I became a writer. Yes, I would absolutely love to tell him, even though, in the end, such a wish only confirms that a part of the little girl I was still lives inside me, intimidated and powerless during those terrible moments, the teacher standing over me, hulking, insistent, heavy—the smell of him insistent and heavy, too. But the terrible moments were just that: moments. Afterward, as soon as he turned around, I went back to my own way, rebellious, determined *not* to write the way he said—the way the Rubio notebooks said!—convinced that my way was much easier and much faster (as confirmed by the language teacher, who never tried to correct me, and by my parents, who couldn't have cared less), making fun of him and his ridiculous math problems that I would eventually manage to copy while holding the pencil correctly.

"A woman goes to the butcher to buy a four-pound chicken. After deboning it and removing the innards, the chicken weighs two-point-eight pounds. If the bones weigh three-quarters the weight of the innards, how much do the innards weigh? And the bones?"

Those problems always made us laugh, especially me and my sister. She'd had the same teacher two or three years earlier, and making fun of him brought me closer to her, made me feel older. Not only was that man obsessed with the right way to hold a pencil, the right way to sit, to make the letters *H* and *J*, to blow your nose, and all the other things that one had to do "the way God intended," he was also fascinated with flesh and viscera, meat and guts, slaughterhouses and butcher shops. He took my sister's class on a field trip to the city abattoir, where they filed through the bloodstained installations and saw the enormous livestock hanging from hooks; my sister came home dumbstruck. When some of the parents complained, the teacher accused them of being soft. He really believed that a person who wasn't strong or brave enough to confront the spectacle of an animal's sacrifice—or the carving of its cadaver—was missing out on the beauty of the body revealed, the calibrated mechanism of muscles, tendons, and bones exposed. The perfection of anatomy, he'd say, enthusiastically displaying his prints of the human body on the lectern. He would bring in the plastic torso from the lab, too, and stick his hand inside with delight, removing the lungs, the heart, the spleen, the liver, showing us up close. This does sound terrifying now—or describing it like this, nowadays, sounds terrifying—but I'm convinced there was nothing sinister about his particular and rather undisguised passion. Rather, he behaved like a young child, not very intelligent and tremendously bent on his own fixations, repeating over and over the theories that, even then, we didn't actually believe, like that the global population ratio was seven women to one man, or, as he said with a wink, "there are seven women for each of us."

Considered broadly, all of that could have been fun. It was fun, in fact. The way we imitated him, and how much we enjoyed ourselves doing it. How easy it was, in the end, to make him ridiculous: his uneven steps, his little pink hands behind his back, our childish voices impersonating his, high-pitched and shrill: "Which weighs more: pork ribs or pork loin? God didn't intend for you to tie your shoes like that! Yawning is forbidden in this class! Will you *ever* be able to hold a pencil properly?"

School and subterfuge, the telephoned threats and my silence, sleeplessness and laughter, a piece of fruit at recess and my good-girl shoes: that was life, it was all that lay ahead, an endless road. Life. Serious and eternal, a path that would lead me, sooner or later, to my sister's age and to friends like hers, boys who seemed almost men to me, boys I liked and who inspired respect. And among them, especially: the redhead, always smiling, always telling jokes, freckled all over—his face, his arms, even his legs—slim and attractive, a real dish, they called him, a delicious dish of carrots, I thought, and I wrote him (and countless others) passionate love letters I later destroyed, since the pleasure lay simply in writing them, in the free flow of bad handwriting from a pencil held my own way.

I don't remember that boy's first name. Just his surname. Mármol, *marble*. A sad paradox.

Nor do I really remember what happened, or the explanation they gave us, if one was given. If one was found. We didn't know it, but the horror dwelled right there, right in the disruption of the norm. We were unfazed by grandmothers jumping off balconies, but why did the Mármol boy do it? Why the kid I now think of as "the Mármol boy," barely fourteen, his laugh, his gestures, that absent gaze and the copper shine of his hair, totally different from the others. The news spread through the halls at school one morning, we said it in a whisper but shouted at the same time—if that's even possible, and it was—we were late returning to our places, taking our seats, each of us at our desk, stunned, unnerved, afraid.

What had happened? And what would happen to us, after his death?

The science teacher entered the room, heavy with sorrow. He didn't say anything: he knew that we knew. He didn't dictate problems that day, or call anyone to the blackboard. He simply made us sit in silence for the hour, a whole hour, in memory of that boy we would never see again. The teacher's face was white and his lips were puckered in a grimace of pain, he scratched his forearms nervously, looked daggers at us if we moved or made a sound. The science teacher, I could see, wasn't a bad guy after all.

The language teacher arrived a little later, her eyes red and hands trembling. She looked at us blankly, smiled weakly. I don't know what to say, she admitted, and burst into tears. Some of us cried with her. There was something tender in that collective grief.

Later, toward the end of the morning, the religion teacher entered the classroom. She was a tall woman, plain, with gray hair. I vaguely remember her feet, big and wide. We didn't know her well because she only taught us once a week. She came in, closed the door, and ordered us to take out our books, to open to page ninety-six. She tried to start the lesson as usual, as if a chasm weren't running through that classroom, as if there weren't a risk that another one of us could fall in. Had no one told her what had happened? We couldn't believe it.

"Teacher," someone said, "don't you know that Mármol committed suicide?"

Suicide. We would have never used that word. Most likely, the boy who dared to speak thought it would be easier to explain himself like that, or believing, perhaps, it was the appropriate word for interrupting class without her getting too angry. The teacher looked up, stared at us, waited a few seconds, preserving the silence, harsh, blunt, taut.

"I know," she finally said.

And then:

"Page ninety-six."

We all opened our books and felt deeply ashamed of something, without knowing what. *Mármol*, I whispered to myself, as if begging forgiveness, and we had class as usual, just as they'd continue to do all the other days at that school, without any other disruptions that I can remember, except, of course, the typical bomb threats, some teacher's retirement, flooding in the portable classrooms—those prefabricated, provisional rooms that eventually became permanent—nothing comparable in the least to what happened to Mármol. The truth is, our lives went on, and, for some time, still seemed eternal. The anomaly, therefore, was nothing more than that: a deviation whose meaning we didn't understand and would never, ever understand. Grandmothers kept jumping from balconies, neatly and methodically. The phone calls stopped and were replaced by another pain, another fear I also saved all for myself. No one gave me a hard time about how I wrote anymore—about how I held my pen or pencil, that is—and, without trouble, I passed each grade. Mármol died and the rest of us survived. Only the memory of it is up for debate. Did the religion teacher really do that? Had she really been so insensitive, so cruel? Or was it merely her own discomfort, her inability to express herself? Had she clung so tightly to her principles—the impossibility of accepting suicide, a human audaciousness before God—that she withheld the compassion owed to a group of kids? Or had she, in fact, said something else, was there some explanation or lament that I can't remember?

Once, I ran into an old classmate and we discussed it. She remembered it more or less the same way I did. We had class as if nothing had happened, she confirmed. The teacher even got mad because we were slow and did poorly on the exercises. I don't think she was a bad person, she added. Just a clumsy woman who didn't know how to handle thirty kids stuck in a classroom. Thirty undisciplined savages. I had to agree.

Then we talked, she and I, about other things. Other misfortunes—accidents, illnesses, unemployment, poverty— as well as occasions for happiness—moves, children, accomplishments that were by turns reasonably obvious or mostly unknown.

"Is it true that you write?" she asked me, laughing.

"Sort of," I said. I always say the same thing, *sort of.*

"What do you write about?" she insisted.

"Oh I don't know, this and that, normal stuff, things I remember or make up."

"Give me an example."

I hesitated.

"Well, after talking to you, I feel like writing about Mármol."

Her eyes widened, surprised.

"But you don't even really remember the details!" she reminded me. "You could get it wrong!"

"No, no . . . not about Mármol, not exactly," I said. "About what life was like then, when the Mármol thing happened. What *my* life was like when the Mármol thing happened." I hurried to correct myself again. "About how I saw it then. A recreation, a fabrication." I saw her relax. "Nothing important."

She remembered perfectly the way I'd held my pencil. "It was horrible!" she said. "Like you had a chicken claw instead of a hand!" Ah, bad handwriting, we both laughed.

As if it were possible to get good handwriting from a twisted pencil.

# JUST A FEW MILLIMETERS

THE FIRST THING I GOT when I walked in, the first impression, I mean, was of being someplace extremely alien and heavy and dark, a sense that went beyond the closed doors and low ceilings and huge quantity of accumulated junk in the entryway as well as in the hallway that the woman immediately invited us to come through, though you wouldn't call it clutter, no, it wasn't that, but more like a lack of space, and of course the need for all that junk—equipment, to be more precise, oxygen tanks and stretchers and other orthopedic devices I don't know the names for—in addition to all a home's usual effects—a shopping caddy, folding stepladder, shoeboxes, cleaning products—all kinds of things heaped everywhere because the dwelling, and this I'd already sensed from outside, was rather small. The woman smiled and her smile went beyond mere politeness, her expression was one of innermost satisfaction that, God forgive me, at first struck me as smugness, though I imagine being smug or proud of that sort of thing isn't normal or healthy or desirable. In any case, she had a big smile on her face, she was genuinely happy

23

to see us, and quickly accepted our apologies for our late arrival—"the traffic"—as she led us down the narrow hallway to the back bedroom, the only room whose door was open, or rather half-open, through which I heard the murmur of a respirator or pump, and sensed a different light, a tint either orange or cloudy, which cast a triangle of light on the floor, as if marking the way in.

The purpose of that light, I later learned, was to get him some vitamin D and lift his spirits, since ultimately, she told us, no matter how hard she tried to get him outside, it was hard, truly hard: it took two hours to get him ready and then another two to get him back in bed after the outing, not to mention the fact that at least two people were required to help move all the equipment on which his life depended; in other words, you needed three people to move him, even though he must have weighed, at most, ninety pounds. As she explained all this, there was no change in her smile, the selfless, sacrificing smile, the smile that does not question the destiny one has been dealt, no matter how bad, and all of a sudden I felt a little embarrassed and lowered my head and realized that that was how I had to enter the sanctum—because it was a sanctum—head bowed, heart ready to acknowledge the suffering that wafted in there and admire the ability to face it.

Now, the learning differences liaison was approaching the boy's bedside. She took his hand in hers and stroked it, speaking to him as sweetly as if he were a little child, this despite the fact that she herself had reminded me on the drive over that, mentally, he was exactly his age, in other words: he was a fifteen-year-old boy with the mind of a fifteen year old.

Or even older, she said, because his confinement has meant that he reads constantly and studies everything he possibly can and this has led him to develop a great intelligence, great intelligence combined with an enthusiastic, curious personality and—though it might seem incredible—an overwhelming desire to live, so make sure you talk to him like you would talk to any of your students, to do otherwise would be hurtful, and I'd nodded as I stared straight ahead, hands on the steering wheel, imagining something very different from what I now had before me. She gestured impatiently.

"Go on, say hi."

"Hello," I whispered.

No change registered in the boy's eyes. They looked, or rather they pointed, at the ceiling, completely devoid of expression; even so, I continued speaking to him, how do you feel, I said, and introduced myself, explaining that I was his Biology teacher and I was there to give him an exam, adding with a smile that he needn't worry, I'd be asking him very simple questions, I was sure he'd know the answers right away. The liaison rushed to clarify that the questions were the same, they were the *exact* same questions the other students would have to answer, he had no reason to feel lesser than anybody, you know that, you are no less than anyone else, she's going to evaluate you just like she evaluates everybody else, and you will get your grade, just like they do.

The boy didn't move his eyes.

The smile still stamped on her face, the mother stood up and asked if she could stay. They'd been studying the list of topics together and she wanted to be present the moment he got his A, since there was no doubt her son would do brilliantly on the exam. The liaison suggested that she ask him what he thought. It's his opinion that counts, she added. Of course, whispered the mother, and looked at her son. She didn't repeat the question. She stared at him and the boy, I could see him doing it, raised his pupils a couple of millimeters, just a few millimeters, and that, apparently, meant "yes." The mother smiled and sat back down.

"See?" the liaison lectured. "He hears all of our conversations, something people often forget."

Then she took out her board with the letters of the alphabet on it, ordered according to frequency of their appearance in Spanish, from most to least common, an order that facilitated the speed of the process, she told me, even though the order they used wasn't based on the latest linguistic research, which situated the e in the first position, along with the articles, prepositions, and conjunctions (such as the omnipresent *que*) she explained, and I thought she must be mistaken but it didn't matter, I got the idea, which was for the boy to dispense with all extraneous elements that complicated communication and to concentrate on the essential words, the most significant, she specified, and so his board began with *a*, followed by *e*, and then *s*, *o*, *r*, *n*, and *i*, notwithstanding, sometimes he was formulating a sequence that clearly demanded a vowel, and then she went straight to them, if for instance the boy signaled to the *p* and then the *l*, a vowel would obviously come next, you see? I nodded and she told me that we'd do a test.

"Do you want to say something to your teacher, honey?"

I didn't think she needed to call him that, *honey*, since as he was just another student like the others, as she so insistently reminded me, it was better for him to know that no teacher would ever speak like that to his or her students, at least no teacher I knew of, and certainly not to a group of fifteen-year-olds. I noted a sense of fear, guilt, and resentment stirring inside of me as I watched the liaison use a pointer to tick off the letters with as much speed as skill, stopping only when the boy raised his pupils to the ceiling, creating a message that started with *h* and ended like this a few minutes later: HELLO TEACHER YOU ARE VERY PRETTY. The liaison set the board on the bed and let out a hearty, indulgent laugh.

"Oh, he has a great sense of humor."

I smiled and looked at him again, though I must admit it was difficult, very difficult, to look at him as if everything was fine, as if it was all totally normal, the squashed, deformed body, the almost-flattened skull, the flaccid arms, the rickety legs under the sheet, even though the liaison had told me the boy was happy with his life and that his existence was a lesson to us all, a "moral" lesson, she said, for us, the rest of us, always complaining about the most trivial things and undermining our own happiness, while he, yes he, settled for what he had, not only did he settle—"settle" wasn't the right word—but he accepted it like a gift and even believed, according to the liaison, that he was fortunate to have been born that way because it let him be who he was, and he never yearned to be anyone else.

That was hard for me to believe, as hard as it was to accept that this wasted, spongy, aged body housed a human being with a sense of humor and who had said *Hello teacher you are very pretty* with his eyes, and I had the fleeting thought, absurd really, that the learning differences liaison was, that she could be, making it all up, that she was fooling us, making us believe that the soulless body before us had feelings, that it reasoned, and communicated, all of it completely made up, the damn board and the sentences it produced like some kind of Ouija game, but I was immediately ashamed of the thought, the expression "soulless body" especially, ashamed that I had literally thought those exact words, soulless body, which was undoubtedly cruel, glaring evidence of my insensitivity and ignorance and inability to empathize, which other people— in other contexts—had thrown in my face, and so I made the effort to believe it all and resolved to love that creature as best as I could. I took out my notebook and announced that I was going to give him the exam. The liaison repeated:

"The same questions as everyone else."

The mother nodded in satisfaction. I acknowledged the statement with a brief nod, the same questions, yes, but it was also true—though obviously I wasn't going to say anything— that the questions were the same because I'd made changes to the regular exam, replacing essay questions with ones that could be answered in a word or two, even making some of them multiple choice, just three possible answers, which I realized—having witnessed the whole eye thing—would simplify things for me. I had also brought a diagram of the human ear, whose parts he had to identify and which we projected on a screen over his head so that he, supposedly, could see it.

We were at it a long time, especially when it came to the diagram, which included too many long words and even compound terms like "eustachian tube," "semicircular canals," "ceruminous glands," and "endolymphatic canals," a good two hours because the boy knew every answer and was set on spelling them out, he wasn't satisfied with CAN or even CANA and insisted on finishing the word, which made it tedious and extremely tense for me, there wasn't enough air in the room, it was too warm, the mother sitting there with arms crossed, smiling, proud of her son, the liaison and her little wand, quick taps on the letters on the board, and me, thinking that their method was clearly anachronistic, that surely a very slight movement of the pupils—the only movement the boy could hope to make—would suffice for some kind of computer to interpret a binary code of communication, or something similar, because even though I don't have the firmest grasp on these things, I'm still sure something faster could be designed. Then I thought: maybe no one has ever considered using a different method, and when I say "different" I mean "better," since that smiling woman, happy in her house chock-full of junk, that poor woman had managed, in short, to get authorities' attention—she'd shown me a few framed pictures of the boy with the mayor, the boy with the education councilor, even one of the boy with a soccer player of some renown—attention she never would have gotten without the unquestionable extent of her misfortune, but attention that was insufficient all the same, superficial and much, much more cut-rate than was required.

"A ninety-seven," I said at last.

"Are you pleased?" the liaison asked the boy.

Eye movement: *Yes.*

The liaison congratulated him and asked if he wanted to tell me anything else. She hadn't put the board down; the pointer remained between her stiff fingers.

CAN YOU RECOMMEND A BOOK FOR ME

"About biology?" I asked.

NORMAL READING

"What do you like?"

EVERYTHING. Then he specified: FANTASY

I thought about how, for him, any book, including the most realistic, was actually fantasy, but quickly regretted my cynicism and recommended Poe's stories. The liaison let out a thin laugh, *ha ha ha* another task for her, the boy, insatiable for new stories, asked for book recommendations from everyone who visited the apartment, but then she was the person who had to read them, since—as she'd explained to me in the car—the mother wasn't a very strong reader, although she had been the one to introduce him to the pleasure of reading—"the pleasure of reading"—mostly by way of children's stories, but then a time came when the boy demanded a level of complexity she couldn't provide and she got tripped up, went too slow, couldn't pronounce the foreign names right, and so now she, the learning differences liaison, took care of it, for instance, she had recited with satisfaction, she'd read him novels by García Márquez and Isabel Allende, which he had really liked, and one by Eduardo Mendoza, which the boy, in his own way, had laughed at nonstop. All in all, she said, good literature, and I had nodded as I kept my eye on the long line of cars on the road ahead.

At that point I openly checked my watch—I'd been discreet before—and announced that we should get going, to which the mother responded with an obsequious *of course* and a new smile even broader than before—the A, I suppose, made her that much happier—and I turned for the last time toward the squashed skull on the pillow, the skull deformed by the position it had been in since birth, the inexpressive mouth, the eyes that were, for the moment, motionless, dull, like a fish's, and mumbled a goodbye and then, even though it was absurd, waited passively with my dumb, compassionate smile for the boy to say goodbye, waited a good long while because the boy was polite and the farewell was a complete one: SEE YOU ANOTHER DAY TEACHER THANKS A LOT FOR COMING.

Outside the apartment, I couldn't resist taking a deep breath.

"It's asphyxiating," I said.

The liaison gave me a long look of reproach.

"Yes, everyone says that."

The drive back didn't take long. The highway was empty at that time of day. We hardly spoke. There was no question, we were both exhausted.


I looked in without knocking; the door was open and the principal isn't usually a fan of formalities. Cradling the receiver on his shoulder, he motioned for me to take a seat, but I refused with a smile and stood there waiting, studying the posters on the walls, the shelves with mementoes of his kids—pictures, drawings—a couple of potted ivy plants, a ridiculous little vase with a paper flower. There was something ostentatious about it all, not in the luxury sense, but in the mere act of putting it all on display, smugly showing it off, and I recalled how this principal frequently made reference to his good taste, not directly, of course, but obliquely, asking our opinion on this or that, isn't it pretty, this bowl I brought back from Morocco, check out this fabulous print I got at the Tate, that sort of thing, and I was suddenly aware, perhaps for the first time, of just how much he rubbed me the wrong way leaving me with the uncomfortable premonition that maybe he'd called me in to chew me out for something I couldn't predict. When he hung up, he looked me in the eyes and used my real name—a name nobody ever uses, as he well knows—and brought up the sex ed talk. The talk? I said. What's up with the talk? We needed to start thinking about arranging the room for the boy to fit, he explained, since he'd be coming with a mobile medical unit and now that the Education Department had approved the budget, we had better get everything ready so that we didn't look bad. Get everything ready? I said, and he insisted, yes, get everything ready, what amounted, he added, to implementing some logistics, an action plan—he was especially fond of that term—and giving the other students a heads up, even though most of them already knew him—individual visits to his home had been organized throughout that semester—and most importantly, giving a heads up to the woman responsible for delivering the talk, the sexologist or psychologist or whatever she was, lock it down, dodge the sort of disastrous outcomes that always catch us off guard, and I sensed hidden criticism of some other issue I couldn't quite put my finger on, so taken aback was I by the shock, such a shock that I couldn't avoid raising my voice a bit, more than I should have.

"Wait, is he really coming for that class?"

"Of course he is. Why not?"

He went on, miffed. He said the language teacher hadn't made a stink when they decided to bring the boy to the theater, and the art teacher had even requested funding for him to visit the engravings exhibit at the Museo de Cárdenas. I swallowed. It's different, I said. The talk had a practical element, it would be focused on preventing unwanted pregnancy—we'd had a few in our high school already—and sexually transmitted diseases, and would address responsible intimate relationships in general, so in my opinion it was an absurdity—"an absurdity" I said, but quickly corrected myself—a *mistake* to bring a boy who would, unfortunately, never get to have a go at sex—maybe I said "be with a girl"—and having him there would be very uncomfortable, it would be baffling, even for him, which was why it had to be avoided, the visit had to be cancelled, it was a mistake, I repeated, a mistake. He raised his eyebrows.

"Neither you nor I are going to ever climb Mount Everest, but we still like to watch other people do it on TV."

"It's different," I insisted.

He crossed his arms and asked why. Why was it different. Could I pinpoint exactly how it was different? He put heavy emphasis on that "exactly," thus forcing me to be more explicit. I said that she was going to explain how to put on a condom, for example, she did a demonstration with a rubber penis,

33

showed them how to roll it down, how to adjust it correctly and avoid an *oops*, I had experienced this scene more than once, the students tended to laugh, elbow each other, there was embarrassment and bravado, it was an odd moment, and what sense did it make for the boy to see it when he would never, ever be able to put on a condom, not correctly, not incorrectly, he had never even been able to touch himself, he didn't have erections—I blushed—it seemed cruel—"cruel" I said—like putting a candy to his lips that he would never be able to eat.

"Cruel?"

The principal's dry laugh was sarcastic and cutting.

"It's crueler to exclude him," he said. He drew himself up to my height. "Fine, so he can't have sex, but there is not a single reason to rob him of that knowledge. Besides, there are things he can do: interact with the other students, laugh with them, have a good time, why not."

"Laugh with them? He can't laugh!"

"Come on! Laughing is more than making noise. You might not be able to understand it, but he *can* laugh."

He looked at me with disgust and I was overwhelmed by a wave of possible retorts, retorts I delivered disjointly, furiously, how could he talk about laughing, if there's no sound how does he know that the boy is laughing, maybe he's crying, how can anyone interpret what the boy feels, but the principal gave me the same response, he said the boy expresses himself just fine, after each activity he always says how it went, what he'd thought, whether he'd liked it or not. He'd done so after the theater, where the show started an hour late because he couldn't see from the box seat he'd been put in and they'd had to lift his stretcher almost ninety degrees, with the added complications of the tubes and all. The show, I thought, had been in the box, not on the stage, but the principal insisted that the boy had had a wonderful time, he said so himself at the end, he liked interacting with his classmates, the principal repeated, and I thought—though I didn't say it—that we could call them what we liked, but "classmates" they were not, no, it was truly idiotic to pretend that the boy went to class with the other kids and had classmates like a normal boy, no, just no, no matter how we tried to dress-up reality, they weren't his classmates, they were just regular kids with regular lives that were nothing like his, and to those kids, the weekly visits to the boy's house were—at best—an uncomfortable obligation, and at worst, a circus attraction.

"He learns everything he needs to learn," I argued. "I don't hide anything from him, no one does. He's known the reproductive system for years. He knows about the human body, every part of it, including the clitoris. I've given him the anatomy tests myself. But this is different. To think that he can participate in everything is pure paternalism. We'll make fools of ourselves."

"Paternalism! You're the one who's paternalistic! Do you know that he asked to come? That his mother is on board? What gives you the right to decide what's good or bad for him? Are you trying to protect him, or yourself?"

And I thought: how could the boy ask to come to the sex talk if someone hadn't offered it to him, and just whose idea was that, and why would he say no, why would his mother say no, if she was all smiles all the time, all gratitude, her whole life centered around getting her son out of the apartment so that people could see him, adore him, and that whole mobile unit enterprise, the nurses sent there on the public's dime, the ambulance, the escape from her asphyxiating routine, all so the boy could watch how to put a condom on, no, how other people—not him—had to put on a condom.

"Following that logic," I argued, "why doesn't he come do the obstacle course at the end of the year?"

"We've thought of that."

They'd thought of that? Was he actually being serious? The boy on an inclined stretcher like a book on a lectern, the flat skull and immobile body, out there in the courtyard watching the other kids running, jumping, throwing water balloons, sparkling, flirting, desiring each other, and meanwhile, he's there moving his pupils a couple of millimeters to say ALL SO VERY FUN? I was momentarily flooded with rage, then giggles, and then I experienced a few seconds of doubt: why did the principal and—according to him—everyone else, the language teacher, the art teacher, why did it all seem so clear to them and so dark to me, there it was again, my damned inclination to see the rotten side of things, those were the exact words said to me once by someone I loved very much, "the inclination to see the rotten side of things," but I also thought about how I had nothing to gain from opposing their wishes, the boy's wishes and those of his mother, according to the principal, who now insisted on stating categorically that the boy would participate in as many activities as possible, that I better get used to it—his nuance was threatening—society better start getting used to it, society at large, society that was uncomfortable with what was different, society that puts blinders on so it doesn't have to see that there are human beings who are different from us, the merry, hedonistic society that won't accept the suffering and sacrifice and vitality of others, the people on the bottom rung, the people it considers unusable, useless, incapable, ugly, he was sermonizing at me, lecturing me, I was perfectly aware of it, but I bowed my head because I thought how there was some truth in his words, in what he was saying about the refusal to look, at least, because I didn't really want to look at the boy, I preferred to pretend he didn't exist, I'd rather he had never been born, and the principal had always had a flair for rhetoric, he spoke well, smoothly articulated his arguments, but I didn't, I was clumsy at expressing myself, I got too anxious, I lacked the vocabulary, and he overwhelmed me, almost convinced me, and yes, I wound up admitting that he was right, maybe I was wrong, I said, though I didn't really believe it, at least not entirely, I'd only had the boy's best interests in mind, I added, but the principal kept talking, he wasn't going to accept any apologies now that he knew he'd won, what was in the boy's best interest was to be part of school life, as difficult as that might be, that was the objective and he wasn't going to let anyone question the objective, case closed, all I had to do was cooperate and stay out of the way, there was nothing more to say, and I said okay, okay I said, okay, and left.

I ran out to my car, an uneasy tickle in my stomach, although as soon as I put the car into gear I forgot the boy entirely, focused only on a flyer that someone had stuck under

.

the windshield wiper, "we cancel fines, consolidate debts, give financial advice, consult our services," they did it all, and I saw that the rain had softened the paper, gluing it to the glass, so that when I turned on the wipers they made a mush of pulp and runny ink, "servi consul adv fine," a paste that only came off, piece by piece, as the car picked up speed on the way toward my house.

All the rest came later. The looks in the hall. The whispers, constant murmurs. She was against it, she was the one who didn't want to do it, it's all her fault, she didn't prepare the students, they should have been briefed, she did nothing, she did everything. And yet, it isn't surprising, what happened. We toed the edge of a cliff and fell off, that was it, that's what I think. The woman in charge of the talk, the sexologist-psychologist-or-whatever, had nodded when I warned her, of course it wasn't a problem, she said, applied psychology in education takes all cases into account, there was nothing to worry about. He can't move anything, I explained, not a single part of his body, his state is very serious, "vegetative," I was about to say, but held back. She made a mollifying gesture, but impatient, too, don't worry, seriously, I've been in worse situations. Worse? I had to laugh. When the boy arrived, I'd studied her, scrutinized her face for any trace of surprise or fear, a twinge of her jaw, maybe, the size of her pupils, and I did it as discreetly as possible, but still, I suppose, a little rudely, and sure enough, she didn't seem to show the slightest reaction to the whole rigamarole, the ambulance in the school courtyard, the nurses gathered around, the stretcher pulled out, the sight of the body in the sunlight as it drew near us, the milky hue more reminiscent of rubber than human flesh, the clickety-clack of metal, the tubes, the mother hovering nearby, the students watching from the classroom windows. And then, in class, the turning heads, the giggles, elbows and shoves, but what was causing them, I wondered, after all, there were always giggles during the talk, it could all be a misinterpretation, except for the fact that the boy was lying there on one side of the room, his presence like some unequivocal reality, propped up on the stretcher but still unable to see everything happening around him, incapable of a chuckle, closed off and enigmatic. The sexologist-psychologist-or-whatever asked questions of the other students, made them participate, encouraged them to talk, ran the Q & A session, and meanwhile the liaison sat beside the boy, at the ready with her board and pointer just in case he was asked if he was aware of male and female contraceptives, if he knew where and how one could get the morning after pill and what its risks were, if he really thought that you couldn't get pregnant when you did it for the first time, ready just in case, but the sexologist-psychologist-or-whatever skillfully wound down the participatory portion of class, she stopped asking questions, now it was straight lecture, dynamic, sure, youthful and relatable, as is usually the case with these sessions. The mother, in the meantime, waited outside on a bench in the hallway, sipping coffee she'd been offered from the teacher's lounge, and the ambulance crew watched the high school girls playing basketball on the shiny new court.

The signs were there, but we didn't know how to see them.

It was the girl who started laughing first, the girl who'd flunked the year before, with her gum, her long earrings, long black hair, long nails, a girl both ordinary and lovely at the same time, her shoulders shook, she didn't even try to hide it, eyes screwed up with laughter, she started laughing when the sexologist-psychologist-or-whatever had gone over to the stretcher so the boy could get a better view of her crude simulation with the penis and the condom—"the prophylactic," she called it—and why shouldn't she laugh, I thought, it was a nervous snigger after all, almost cathartic, it was probably inevitable, somebody had to, we were all on edge, everyone except maybe the learning differences liaison, sitting with her board primed and ready, and if she had just stayed quiet, if we all, I thought, had just kept up the charade like it was no big deal, pretended we hadn't heard the girl laughing, but no, the liaison just had to stand up, had to go over to the girl—a lioness, as I knew well by then—and challenge her, ask her what the problem was, what she was laughing about, what was so funny, shouting right at her, at the lioness, who shot right back—she wouldn't shut up, she never shut up—with what we were all were thinking, why bother showing the boy if he was never going to be able to do it.

"We don't know what life has in store for us—maybe you'll get hit by a bus and won't get to do it either."

The girl slapped her thigh.

"Ho ho okay," the girl said. "I've already done it tons of times! And baby, it was worth it!"

The peals of laughter were spreading now, an uproar, a tide of voices, of cackles, rebukes and whistles, and I jumped to my feet as well, told the girl to be quiet, while the sexolo-gist-psychologist-or-whatever stood open-mouthed, condom in hand, the rubber penis still unsheathed, and the liaison raised her voice, you ought to be ashamed, and the girl, what do you want me to say, teacher, I feel bad for the dude, what do you mean, you feel bad? you're going to be expelled for what you've said, and another voice from the back of the room, the cocky kid, the boyfriend, maybe, or one of the many boys who hung around the lioness, defending her, lion, peacock, cock-of-the-woods himself, with his war cry, but teacher, she's right, dude can't even jerk off, why the fuck did you bring him here?

*Why the fuck did you bring him here.* The words we pre-tended not to hear resounded in the classroom.

Then came the silence. A silence deep and fleeting that quickly yielded again to confusion, like the interrupted breath of a sleep apnea sufferer, snorting awake.

I kicked the couple out of class. The boy's mother saw them leave, smiled at them because she had no idea what had hap-pened inside, although it's possible that even if she had known, she would've smiled just the same, generous and understanding. The liaison and the sexologist-psychologist-or-whatever took turns manifesting their indignation, their small, value-added contribution to the lecture, and even I slipped in a sentence or two, this can't be, we have to work harder for equality, no one should laugh at anybody else, we all have the same rights, while the students settled down, some of them frankly em-barrassed by what had happened, scandalized by the couple's rudeness or, at minimum, prepared for class to resume so it could all be forgotten as quickly as possible, glancing at the boy who remained on his stretcher as if he'd heard nothing, knew nothing, showing no sign of anything at all.

Once everyone had quieted, the talk resumed. A half hour later, it was over.

The principal was waiting by the door, chatting with the mother, that is, talking to the mother, who nodded anxiously with the look of someone trying to understand and not quite managing it. The stretcher was wheeled out and everyone swirled around the boy, and by everyone I mean the sexologist-psychologist-or-whatever, the liaison, two or three teachers from the adjacent classrooms, and me. I remember that a ray of light was filtering in through a skylight. It fell on the boy's face, right in his eyes, and I thought maybe it would be bothersome when he moved his pupils, but no one said anything and neither did I. The liaison took out her board and stroked his hair, which was very straight and balding at the back where his head met the pillow. She took a breath and asked him the customary question: how was it? A series of letters followed, *a*, *e*, *s*, *o*, *r*, *n*, the swift rap of the pointer, the message taking shape in our heads, the message that returned us to normalcy, REALLY GOOD LIKED IT ALL LEARNED A LOT.

"Anything else?"

Board and the pointer still in hand, the liaison leaned gently over the boy and the sexologist-psychologist-or-whatever, maternal now, stroked his hand with her fingertips, an evasive, noncommittal touch. The pupils.

GRACIAS

The principal looked at me out the corner of his eye. He didn't have to say anything: the look itself contained his resounding victory. I felt it taking root, the culpability, paradoxical because I knew that, even if I did the exact opposite, if I said the opposite and practiced the opposite and even thought the opposite, I would never be rid of that guilt because it was collective, Guilt with a Capital G, the guilt of health in the presence of illness, or taking it a step further, the guilt of life in the presence of death, a guilt that pulsed, in check, in the space of just a few millimeters, I'd even say, if it didn't sound so solemn and so trite and, at the same time, so inescapably true.

# "CREAMY MILK AND CRUNCHY CHOCOLATE"

ONE DAY—ONE NIGHT—an elderly couple died because of me. It happened on Los Infantes Avenue around nine o'clock. If you aren't familiar with Cárdenas, suffice it to say that Los Infantes is a wide and fairly heavily-trafficked road, with two lanes traveling in both directions, a so-called "city artery." Even so, the problem that day wasn't traffic but low visibility. Night was falling, it was drizzling, and a kind of fog of raindrops and car exhaust floated in the air. That was the state of things when, as I was driving home, I saw the two of them standing on the median. I took pity on them, stopped, and gestured with my hand for them to cross. They crossed and the car that was traveling on my right, who couldn't see them, passed me and ran them over. The man was killed immediately and the woman, who was very badly injured, died a week later. No matter how often my friends tell me that it wasn't my fault—the couple shouldn't have been crossing there, after all—the truth is, I did hasten their deaths when I stopped and let them go. Surely, if I hadn't done so, they would have stayed on the median until the road was clear and they could cross no problem. Not even my most understanding friends can deny that.

The elderly couple's family—their children—wanted me to be held accountable for reckless endangerment, though in the end they didn't bring a formal suit. My lawyer told me that, after thinking it through, they had accepted the deaths for what they were, a "terrible accident," as they say. They didn't blame me. Their parents were very old, their sight was bad, they were clumsy walkers, and the family couldn't completely understand what they were doing there on the median at that time of night. My action had been irresponsible, without a doubt, but it wasn't the sole cause of the events.

I could admit all of that as well, but my own remorse had less to do with that part of the drama and more with the driver of the other car, the one who ran them over and technically killed them. Now, he hadn't been to blame at all. He had been driving at a reasonable speed, in his lane, there was no reason for him to stop where there was no sign telling him to do so. And so, out of nowhere, because of my poor decision, his life was forever changed when he rammed into them. I won't go into detail about how unpleasant the scene was and the state of his car after that, but you can guess: if I still think about it daily, I don't even want to imagine the torture it must be for him.

He was a little older than me, and looked like a humble, good-natured guy. He lowered his head when he spoke, suffering real pain from being involved in the situation. I saw him cry. Several times. He never reproached me, not even once. When I apologized—which I did insistently over the days that followed—he simply looked at me with a look of absolute devastation. He couldn't be consoled. It didn't matter what I, or anybody else, said. His wife, on the other hand, did seem truly annoyed. She didn't even want to speak to me when I tried to approach her. The only time we passed in the hospital hallway where the old woman was dying, she quickened her pace and stepped aside. Then she watched me from a distance, her arms crossed, defiant. She was a bony woman, very tall, with the air of a strong personality. Later, one morning in the early hours, she called me on the phone and, in a voice rough with rage, she requested—no, she *demanded*—that I never speak to her husband again, her husband whose life I had "completely ruined." She also said that if I was looking to clear my conscience, I needed to do it somewhere else, because every time that I asked her husband how he was doing, he sank even lower because of me. Therefore, not only had I brought about the deaths of the poor elderly couple—she didn't say "brought about the deaths of," she said "killed"—but if I continued down that path I was going to finish off her husband and father of her son, emphasizing the last part: *my son*.

I'm just asking for a little respect, she added. He's so depressed that he's capable of doing something stupid.

I found that chillingly reasonable and knew that by using the expression "doing something stupid" she wasn't exaggerating even a bit. I obeyed and didn't call him again. Curiously, I felt comforted: I saw that he had a wife who cared about him, somebody willing to bare her teeth—and bite, if necessary—to defend him.

Even so, the discomfort continued. "Discomfort" is a weak term, but it's an apt one for how I felt at the time. It wasn't a constant malaise that impeded me from living my life, but more of a pinch of uneasiness that harried me on occasion, something very bothersome. For example, I felt bad if I laughed in public. I've always been a real joker, I love word play and telling jokes, but now I had to curb my impulse to do it. I also found myself forced to exaggerate my show of sadness: I stopped going to the movies with my friends and my walks with the dog were reduced to the strictly necessary, and, whenever possible, to the ugliest, most somber streets. Even if an important part of me had, as they say, "turned the page," another part told myself that it wasn't okay to forget so soon, and that my behavior couldn't be so inconsiderate. I pretended, but I felt bad for pretending. Or to put it another way: I felt bad for not feeling worse.

This is nothing but a manifestation of your guilt complex, my sister said. Deep down, you still haven't forgiven yourself.

My sister was the one who recommended I go to therapy, even though she knew that I've always considered psychology, sessions, workshops, all those self-help groups, to be nothing but another ridiculous form of religious belief. I concealed my skepticism so as not to offend her—she's a psychotherapist herself—and accepted her advice. She told me about a special group that, she said, was dedicated to treating "the guilt complex." The goal was to rehabilitate using methods similar to those employed in treating addiction: confession and the pooling of sins in order to achieve a certain degree of relief or sedation—dogma! Everyone, therefore, told the story that tormented them and the rest convinced him or her in unison that no, no, no, some things just happen without anybody necessarily being the cause.

I met Braulia in one of those sessions. Braulia is an awful name for a woman, I know, but you had to have seen her: she's sweet, appetizing, almost magnetic, although she would undoubtedly be even more so if she didn't live martyred by regrets. Her situation isn't one of the worst ones—her clinical situation, I mean—but it also isn't the best, although classifying the cases according to those criteria—better or worse with respect to *what?*—is obviously useless. One of the first things I learned here is that the suffering that produces guilt is almost never equivalent to the dimensions of the tragedy. Nor the *self-blame*. The guilt complex isn't guided by rational "parameters": its logic is *intrinsic* and based on false and difficult-to-assign *premises*.

As you can see, I absorbed the theory, but don't go thinking that I understood it all. It was enough for me to listen and take vicarious comfort in other people's misfortune. The majority of people who attended the meetings were besieged by the pain of blaming themselves for events they had no responsibility for whatsoever. This was the case with the woman who believed that abandoned dogs—all dogs—were run over and killed because she didn't pick them up. And so she was responsible for every one she saw—she always tried to catch them and bring them to the pound, where, curiously, she knew nothing of their fates—but also for the ones she didn't see. Frequently she got in the car and combed the city streets and alleys, looking for dogs. For her, guilt didn't reside with the people who abandoned them—she was incapable of going back to that moment in their life stories—nor the other drivers—who spotted the dogs on the side of the road and drove on with no problem—but with her, only her, given that she was, essentially, *the person who should protect them* and didn't. Another boy suffered intensely when food went bad. His mother bought huge quantities of food and didn't know how to manage it well, and so they often had to throw out what had expired or gone bad. He cried, threw himself on the floor, kicked. He couldn't understand how he could have allowed such a horror to occur. To him, it represented the embodiment of the mortality of the flesh, or something like that, an idea that caused him almost existential anguish. Patients like these had something more complex than a simple sense of guilt—obsessions, serious mental disorders, or other pathologies about which I have no idea—but still they came to the sessions to listen or talk about their cases. More common were stories like one about a woman who felt responsible for the firing of a colleague whom she had filled in for during her leave—she had done such a good job that the bosses had seen the ineptitude of the woman she was substituting for—or the man who thought he was responsible for his son's brain damage because he didn't bring him to the hospital when his fever started to spike. It mattered little to the man that the medical reports certified that the same damage would have occurred no matter how fast he reacted, just as it mattered little to those who feared to swindle their parents, children, or partner out of any kind of forgiveness.

And Braulia? She didn't talk much. She sat in a corner,

beside the window. The light fell on her hair, lightening it, sharpening her tormented profile by highlighting her fine nose and sharp cheekbones. She chewed her lip and bit her nails constantly, and from time to time she would blink quickly, squeezing her eyes tight, as if she wanted to erase a memory and start from zero. Behind her, through the window, you could see the path leading to the building, flanked by jacaranda trees that carpeted the ground with their withered blossoms. Farther beyond, the irregular line of rather coarse buildings with large parabolic antennas, and a huge Heineken billboard, dominated over everything. I watched her discreetly and sought strategies to speak to her as we left the meeting. I imagined myself walking away down the path with her, with the billboard in front of us, the blocks of buildings silhouetted against the sky. When I think about those days, hazy purple and green images come to mind, a possible blend of the jacarandas and the light from the billboard as the sun set, something similar, I guess, to nostalgia. Braulia wasn't young at that point—I wasn't either—but her innocence overwhelmed me. I asked myself how such a being, so pure, so untouched, could feel guilty of anything.

I didn't learn her story until the seventh session. It was a strange day, the room charged with an electric tension that corrupted the atmosphere. It was impossible to be bored, even though the attention we paid was superficial and intermittent. One girl shook as she told us about her boyfriend, whom she had recently left. She said she was afraid he would commit suicide and, of course, she felt *really guilty* about it. As she spoke, she raised her extremely thin arms up toward the ceiling, histrionic. She gestured in a horrible way. We all overacted like that, but she was excessive. We got even more anxious. Braulia came out of her lethargy and started to shiver. Her teeth chattered. She hugged herself, hunched over her knees. The therapist gave her the floor. What's wrong, Braulia, she said. What's going on with you? Braulia didn't reply. Do you want me to tell the others your story? Maybe it would help our friend here. Maybe it would be good for you to tell it. Braulia stopped shaking. Now she simply looked frightened. She made a gesture of refusal. But the therapist spoke.

She spoke about a suicide. A woman's suicide. Her husband had been Braulia's lover—that was the word she used, "lover." She spoke about the elements that were producing confusion: the feeling of jealousy, of abandonment. She spoke of the consequences that were not Braulia's responsibility: two orphaned children, a family destroyed. She explained that the woman had already tried, on several occasions, so Braulia didn't *really* form part of the story's nucleus. In fact, her state of depression was, in part, what had "driven her husband into the arms of another woman"—those were her exact words. Hence, was there a guilty subject in this case? And if there was, did anybody actually believe it was sweet Braulia? She pointed toward the corner and Braulia lifted her ashamed gaze, showing no hint of relief. Before the eyes of God—and she was a believer, a real believer—she was guilty and there was no possible atonement for her mistake. Sputtering, she said that when she thought of the orphans, she couldn't stop crying. As for her lover, she had stopped seeing him immediately, and had inflicted physical harm—including burns—on herself as punishment. She swore that never, ever again would she be carried away by lasciviousness.

Lasciviousness? asked a fellow participant. He thought the term was too harsh. Why not call it a need for affection, search for closeness, or just plain love? She was hurting herself if she thought of it like that, as lasciviousness. Braulia didn't respond, except to add a synonym: lust. I looked at her and thought that she was the least lustful-looking person in the world.

I approached her by the exit and offered to walk with her for a bit. She asked me if I was married. No, I told her, which was true. Together we walked the little path that I had so often stared at through the window. Swifts crossed above our heads, shrieking madly. Perhaps they weren't the best start, those caws, but I could sense that it was good for her to walk alongside me. That's how it all began.

I won't say it was easy. It wasn't. Braulia thought she had no right to fall in love with someone she met as a result of somebody else's suicide. She linked all the events with a twisted logic: if she hadn't "contributed to adultery"—her words—she would have never found herself in that tale of obsession and guilt, she would never have found me. She should restrict herself to attending church—where she went to confession every week—and not getting involved with that group of loony and "immoral moderns" who tried to justify their "sins" at all costs and who, with the group as excuse, did nothing but look for "new occasions to sin." Some nights, she listened to a radio program featuring an American-style preacher, a program that lasted for hours and hours and which she listened to with her eyes closed, head slightly bobbing. When the attacks overcame her and her sense of guilt was exacerbated, she adopted that manner of expression—the preacher's manner—and became more and more worked up. Then I would hold her tightly in my arms, stroke her hair, and whisper in her ear whatever occurred to me, anything at all. It worked. She calmed down. Another Braulia sprang from her, younger, healthier. It was a kind of challenge for me: get to know the woman she had been before she was beaten down by illusions of guilt. Rescue her. Save her from torment. I now had a mission in life. I no longer thought about the man who ran over the elderly couple because of me. I was completely over the part I'd played in the story. I laughed in public again, told jokes. Sometimes my laughter was contagious for Braulia. And it was comforting to feel this: the existence of a more or less clean path ahead.

Everything was—everything is—however, too fragile in life. And there are small instants, epiphanies, revelations, images that open up, words that split apart. Sometimes it happens, and then something breaks and everything changes. This happened to me as well, one afternoon.

It was at the grocery store. I saw him there, shopping with a little boy. From the child's age and the way the man spoke to him, guiding him with his hand lightly on the back of the boy's neck, I knew right away it was his son. They went placing items in their cart with a certain seriousness. It was an ordinary scene, but at the same time, very solemn. I waited in a corner and observed them. I didn't see any sign of suffering in the man. He looked better than when I met him. Too serious or reflective, maybe, although I had the impression he was a person prone to introspection regardless, independent of what might have happened to him in the past. I followed them until they finished shopping and went to the checkout to pay, and then I felt the impulse to know more—the need to know more—and I abandoned my basket in the aisle, left the store while continuing to watch them out of the corner of my eye, got in my car, and waited for them to finish up. If they had also come by car, I thought, I'd follow them in mine; if they'd walked, I would follow them on foot. I didn't even ask myself why. My attention was focused solely on seeing them exit through the automatic doors and left room for nothing else. They appeared a few minutes later. I saw him push the shopping cart toward a car—a new car, smaller, white—and unhurriedly load all the bags into the trunk. He also took his time settling the child in the back seat, making sure his seatbelt was fastened correctly. They were easy to follow: he drove slowly, respecting all road signs. He stopped at intersections even when it wasn't necessary, made scrupulous use of the turn signal before any change in direction. I was happy to see him driving, because I had heard him say that he would never do it again. Braulia had thought, as well, that she would never be able to sleep with another man, and yet. Even I had believed, for a time, that I wouldn't be able to laugh again, to be the same as I was before, and yet. Life goes on, I thought, and then I wondered why they went so far to do their shopping—I'd been following behind them for a good long while—when there were so many grocery stores so much closer. Ten minutes later, I parked in a small plaza, a certain distance from where he had parked.

The little plaza had a slide and a set of rickety teeter totters. The man helped the boy out of the car, took his hand, and they went over to the playground in silence. I stayed inside my car. They didn't see me, but I could make them out clear as day. The scene didn't seem as natural to me now. There was tension in the way the boy rocked and watched his father, and also in the way the man repeatedly checked his watch and pushed back his hair with his hand. He looked nervous. He took out a handkerchief and wiped his forehead. It wasn't warm out, but when he raised his arm to lift his son, I noticed the sweat stains under his arms. They were the only two people in the little park. Suddenly, that seemed strange and sad: the boy, the father, the worn playground equipment, the dirty clay surface, the absence of words, the repeated glances at his watch. I also saw him check his phone, scan one of the apartment buildings that surrounded the plaza a few times, as if expecting to find something or someone. It remained deserted. The boy got off the teeter-totter and went over to his father and leaned against his legs. The man made a vague movement, as if to hug him, but stopped short. Then he crouched down beside the boy and whispered in his ear. They went back to their car. The man took something out from one of the bags in the trunk and handed it wordlessly to the boy. The child shook his head. The man seemed to insist. Clear as day the boy shouted: *I don't want it!* and the man slammed the trunk shut, throwing whatever it was—I couldn't see from that distance—on the ground. Then he took the boy's hand and led him toward the apartment block he had looked over. I got out of my car to follow. From behind, I saw that they had the same way of walking: slightly hunched, toes turned outward, head bowed. I understand it in the father, but did the child also feel defeated? I don't know where that thought came from. Defeated? A boy of, I don't know, seven or eight? *Defeated?* Simply from his way of walking?

They stopped at the main entry to the building and buzzed the intercom. They stood stiffly, in silence, looking at the ground. I got closer than I should, thinking that, even if he were to see me, he wouldn't recognize me. All the positive signs I thought I'd seen in the grocery store were vanishing now, and before me was a troubled man, beaten down, with ruddy skin and trembling hands. Then the door opened and I saw her, his wife, just as bony as before, just as resolute, she was like a gust of air that grabbed the boy and swept him inside, leaving the man alone outside by the door, where he remained for several seconds without moving. Then he looked up and saw me. I couldn't tell if he recognized me. His eyes were as hollow as a dead and stuffed animal's. Cowardly, I turned away. I turned around and made my way back down the path and was incapable of confronting that look that maybe wasn't hollow, but furious, or perplexed. I retraced my steps at a jog and, as I passed his car, saw what the child had spurned. It was candy. *Creamy milk and crunchy chocolate*, I read. I don't know how I had time to read it. Remembering it now, the image is crystal-clear, the orange and white packaging, the yellow and blue letters, the glint of the wrapper tossed beside the tire. I sped up. I wanted to cry.

Everything comes apart in an instant, or the span of a few minutes, ten or fifteen minutes, not many more, the same amount of time it took me to drive to Braulia's place and ring the bell while something harsh and extremely unpleasant rose in my throat. And then she opened the door, looked at me with surprise, held out her arms as I threw myself on her. Right there in the foyer, where I almost collapsed—and that was guilt, *that* and not the weak tickle I'd felt for months—I asked her to kneel with me, I asked her to pray with me to that God she believed in, I yearned to believe in Him and receive his absolution and solace, and I knew that it wasn't that I had a mission in Braulia, but the opposite, that she was rescuing me from indifference.

Later, hours later, after we prayed, and made love, and prayed again, when we were still trembling and night had long fallen, implacable, over the immensity of our guilt, I remembered that I had forgotten the dog at the grocery store entrance, tied up at the bike rack where I usually left her while I shopped, and I rushed back as fast as I could, but they'd already taken her—someone had taken her—and when I called the pound, praying—praying again—for her to be there, the answering machine picked up and informed me that "business hours were from 9 A.M. to 2 P.M. and 5 to 7 P.M.," and I was very familiar with the pound, and I knew that all the professionalism coming through the voice on the answering machine was a farce, and that the sterile tone didn't cancel out the filthy cages or the smacks with a stick or the scarcity of food or the barking of sick dogs, and that was one of the longest, and hardest, nights of my life.

# STONEWORDS

I'D WISHED FOR THE ceiling lamp to fall on her for so long that sometimes I think that it really happened, that it came right down on her head. But it never did. The lamp was already a little loose; one side had pulled a few centimeters away from the ceiling, something no one had realized and which I certainly wasn't going to point out. Of course, there was the risk that if it did come completely away and fall that it would also hurt my uncle, but I considered that possibility unlikely because he rarely ever slept in their bed. My aunt, on the other hand, slept there every night and for long afternoon naps, as well, complaining of migraines. It was simply a question of waiting for the miracle to occur.

Back then, I believed that by wishing for something with great intensity I could make it happen, that the harder I wished, the more likely it would come true, and so, being an essentially realistic young person and knowing that my desire also put my uncle in danger, I wished for the lamp to kill her but, at most, only slightly injure him. It was a heavy lamp made of pieces of green glass held together by a bronze frame, glass hexagons at the center and triangles at the base, where it narrowed in the shape of a teardrop. I remember it now in such precise detail because I spent hours scrutinizing the space between the top of the fixture—a heavy, solid cylinder corroded by the damp—and the plaster ceiling—yellowing, most likely weak—gauging whether or not this gap was growing over time. Given that the lamp hung directly over her chest, I believed my aunt had no chance of surviving. This was not the only way I imagined her death.

Sometimes, for instance, I wished she would crash her old Renault 5 into a wall. I specifically imagined the wall at the entrance to our street, where you had to maneuver a bit at the turn. It was a brick wall on which someone had painted *NO LAYOFFS AT BOCAL* and, in English, *FUCK MAY 68 FIGHT NOW*, which I read thousands of times in those days, ignorant of what "fuck" or "Bocal" meant. In any case, it was more likely that she'd die crushed by the lamp than smashed up against that graffiti because my aunt rarely took the car and when she did, she was a very careful driver. She drove slowly and raged at anyone who passed her, especially kids on mopeds. The other possibilities I eventually ruled out—a frying pan filled with boiling oil, ruthless robbers breaking into the apartment, an earthquake, a flood—were also uncertain and improbable. At nine years old I was, as I said, essentially realistic.

Tinker always told me to relax. Relax a little, he'd say, you shouldn't think like that at your age, what are you saving for later? He didn't know that my aunt had him in her sights, too: she was always badmouthing him, like she did pretty much everyone, but especially about him. Why are you hanging around with that man, she'd say, why don't you spend time with girls your own age, what are you doing with that old cripple? I didn't want Tinker to know that she called him *that old cripple* because he'd already suffered enough, and because it was true, he *was* old—forty, at least—and he *was* crippled—from the accident—but also because he was kind and knew a lot about cartoons and always warmed up little squares of chocolate in the sun before putting them in bread for an afternoon snack. When I tried to explain all this to my aunt, she said that the old pervert—I didn't know then what "pervert" meant—had no reason to be making me snacks and certainly no reason to sit and watch TV with me, and forbid me from seeing him. After I started sneaking off on my bike when she'd leave to do the shopping, she took the bike and gave it to some gypsies. You're going to end up just like your mother, she always said, and my uncle shares the blame for this too, because he never defended me. One time, he even showed up at Tinker's house and right there in the doorway—he refused to enter even though Tinker invited him inside—grabbed me by the arm like I had done something wrong and told Tinker to leave me alone. He even threatened to go to the police, *what was an old guy doing with a young girl*, parroting my aunt's words, carrying out her orders, *what kind of friendship is this*, and all the rest. Tinker didn't defend himself. He told me to go with my uncle, said I needed to obey him. And though he seemed to be a little sad, he didn't even look at me as I walked away.

Tinker was, at least at the time, my best friend. The only

person who spoke well of my mother. Everybody else either went quiet or insinuated bad things about her. Some of them closed their eyes, as if it hurt them to remember her. Others pursed their lips, or glanced away. They looked at me with pity and patted my head. *You poor little thing, at least you have your aunt and uncle.* None of this hurt me. Not anymore. It annoyed me more than anything, the repetition of it all. I liked that Tinker was different. He told me that my mother was very beautiful—he said it naturally, like when someone says that a dog is cute or that the stars are brighter than usual—and he also told me that she was generous and shared what she had with everyone else, that she was always laughing and loved cats and had the same dimple on her chin as me and Silvio. I asked my aunt about the dimple, if it was true that we had gotten it from my mother—neither she nor my uncle had one—and she said Tinker was an old cripple with no respect. I didn't see the connection between being an old cripple and remembering my mother's dimple, but I decided it was better to keep quiet. The first thing a girl of a certain age should learn—by then I'd turned ten—is to keep quiet. Silvio, on the other hand, didn't know how to shut up. He asked about our mother a lot more than I did, and when he did my aunt gathered him in her arms and cooed at him between deep sighs, even though it was obvious that he was looking for answers, not comfort. In contrast, such questions made my uncle very nervous. He'd say, *shh, shh,* let sleeping dogs lie. That was one of his favorite expressions: let sleeping dogs lie. Don't bring it up, don't talk about it, let sleeping dogs lie.

In the end, we were left with very little understanding about what had happened. We had to make do with speculation, rumors, sentences we sometimes half-overhead in the darkness of the living room after we'd already been sent to bed.

*Disgusting. It's obviously in your blood.* At ten-almost-eleven years old I didn't really understand what my aunt meant by this either, and I didn't want to. I had hidden some magazines under my mattress, magazines a school friend (a "repeater" who'd been held back a grade) had lent me and which featured handsome singers (eye candy, the Repeater said), a fashion spread with pictures of dresses I would never, ever be able to buy, and a kind of relationship column where girls could write to a Miss Lingerie with questions like "when are you ready to stop being a girl and give yourself completely as a woman," or if it was true that "by touching yourself you could get a tingly feeling," and that "you didn't need a boy to explore your own body." I remember those questions perfectly, but not Miss Lingerie's answers, which were incomprehensible to me. Nor have I forgotten my aunt's face when she spat out the word *disgusting*, and threw them all in the trash. She picked up the magazines by their corners with two fingers, like they would stain her. And then, her voice on the verge of turning into a scream, she said if I carried on like that then it wouldn't be long before I'd get myself knocked up. I'd already heard the expression before, but never in reference to me: look at Chico's girl, she got herself knocked up. Or: she said she went to the city to find work, but really she didn't want people to know she was knocked up. Or: girls these days have no shame about getting married after getting knocked up, proud as peacocks in their tight dresses, no veils hiding their faces. I felt so horrible that as soon as she turned her back I knew I had to run away, the urge was so strong that I didn't even care about the tongue-lashing I'd get later. I made for Tinker's house. He wasn't home so I went to look for him in the bar, but he wasn't there either, so I waited for him on the side of the road where the orchards began. No luck, so I went back to his house and sat on the front step, crying and hugging my knees as night fell until my aunt—not Tinker—showed up with my uncle following sadly behind. She grabbed me by the arm and snarled: I knew you would be here. You're really asking for it, aren't you? Just like a whore. That was the first of many times that she would use that stoneword against me, not even as an insult but simply describing an undeniable fact, coldly and consciously.

The Repeater's mother did not consider this normal. My friend had told her everything: the magazines, me being forbidden to see Tinker, the bike. My aunt and uncle were not at all normal, she told me, because things weren't like that anymore. Fortunately, society was changing, she assured me as she mixed my chocolate milk. She herself, she said, *she herself* was a good example of those changes. A woman wouldn't even dream of getting divorced before. You wouldn't even dare to think about it, much less if you had a daughter. But she had done it and everything turned out okay, she knew how to take care of herself, she didn't need a man. I wasn't so sure about that—that everything had turned out okay—because people said the divorce was precisely the reason her daughter got held back in school. Girls deserve the same freedom as boys, she said later. We're all equal. But what if the boys didn't have any freedom, either? I thought. Because Silvio, young as he was, found himself forced to live a double life, too. He was yelled at, forbidden from hanging out with the downstairs neighbor kids, from playing soccer, buying candy, watching *Mazinger Z*. Although I wasn't really impressed with what the Repeater's mother said, it wasn't worth arguing about and I agreed with her as I drank my chocolate milk. I'd just turned twelve and had already developed the maddening ability to argue over everything, to consider everything from all possible angles, without even having to open my mouth. You come over here when your aunt gets annoying and we'll talk about girl stuff, the Repeater's mother laughed, whatever "girl stuff" was. Then she went off to watch her soap opera and smoke one cigarette after another, as I watched her with the mistrust that was becoming such an ingrained part of me.

Was my life really so awful? I envied the Repeater's life, but still, I had my doubts. It's true that we had restrictions, always, and fights, of course, but sometimes my aunt laughed—her laugh was lovely—and sometimes my uncle played cards with us—he was tireless, like a little kid—and on a good day the kitchen would become a safe place, with Silvio being silly and the three of us laughing as he threw himself into his antics, wrapped in the smell of the warm potato omelet, the recently-watered plants, damp earth. Everything seemed solid then and we felt curiously good, like a normal family, at least for a little while. Why couldn't that feeling last forever? I looked at myself in the mirror, at my lanky, ugly body, bad hair, big feet, knobby knees, and I felt so out of place, so removed from everyone, the chance of ever being better or changing so unlikely that the same old ghosts would begin to stir again. My uncle shouting for me at the top of his lungs, again. My aunt complaining about me being late, being dirty, again. Again, the demands, the innuendos, the stonewords, the isolation, all of it again and again and stronger every time, as the days passed and I grew up.

Things got worse. Tinker only waved to me from a distance now. He wouldn't let me come near him if there were people around, and there were always people around. He never touched me or lifted me in his arms like before. I started to think that the distance between us didn't upset him very much. I wasn't the same little girl and he looked older and more tired every day. Things with the Repeater weren't much better. When I didn't pass English or math, my aunt forbade me from hanging out with her. I argued that she had no cause to stop me, given the fact that even though I'd failed, I still knew a lot more math and English than she did, and she called me disrespectful and grounded me for two weeks. *Who cares*, I said out loud in English, *nothing ever changes, and you are an ugly bad woman* and she grounded me for three weeks. Mouthing off wasn't going to help, but I couldn't help it. Anger and spite weren't solutions either, I knew that already, but there they were, beating hard beneath the hurt. What else could I do?

Things got even worse. For the first time, Silvio and I weren't allowed to go to the retreat in the woods organized by our school. According to my aunt, that trip wasn't a retreat or anything of the sort. It was just an excuse, but she didn't explain what for. She said that I didn't need to be hopping around in a burlap sack or getting my T-shirt wet with water balloons at thirteen years old. Then she started in on the story she had told us a thousand times, the one about the teacher arrested for bringing kids to his house and doing *God-knows-what* with them, which led her to my friendship with Tinker, *that old cripple*, then the time she found the magazines, and the Repeater, and the failed classes, then back to the retreat in the woods. This sequence could wind up lasting hours, or even days, it became circular, turning around and around on itself, driving us crazy. Something new could always be added to the chain, but she never, ever took anything away.

The lamp hadn't moved a single millimeter in all that time. The days when I had wished so fervently for it to fall seemed long in the past. I learned that the intensity of my desire was not enough. Even my greatest efforts came to nothing. At fourteen years old, locked in my room, sprawled on my bed, I squeezed my eyes shut so tight that red stains formed behind my eyelids, bright circles that grew and receded. Nothing happened. I pressed harder until shapes of black and blue appeared and my teeth ground down from the pressure, my neck and jaw stiff. Nothing happened. Focused, insistent, I wished that Tinker's nephew would look at me, walk by me and look at me just once, turn his head even a little, or his eyes at least, and look at me, even if only to show that he was aware of my presence. Nothing happened. He never looked at me, despite my longing, my need, my angst, despite the spots behind my eyes and the gnashing of teeth. I was devastated to learn that no, wishing wasn't enough.

One spring day at recess, crushed by boredom and the heat of the sun, I walked up to the classmate everyone called Chino and kissed him on the lips. I kissed him quickly, desperately, because I knew if I kissed him he wouldn't pull away, and because Tinker's nephew was nearby and maybe it would make him look at me—it did—but Julia, the teacher's daughter, also saw me and she must have told her mother. Her mother told my aunt, who let loose another string of those stone-words that at fifteen years old I was used to hearing and which slid over my ears, my arms, my legs, not even catching me by surprise. It was always the same in the end: one stoneword after another, justifying the confinement, the control, the inspection of notebooks and mattresses, the tally of how much time I spent studying, the overprotection—the goddamn overprotection—and the determination to direct me down the right path. There's still time, I heard her say, there's still time for her to change, to be better.

Maybe that's the reason Julia became so important in my life that day, the day I kissed Chino. Julia, oh such lovely dark eyes, why don't you hang out with Julia, Julia is learning to play the piano, she has patience, Julia is smart because she does music and on top of it she gets good grades, she looks after her little brother, she looks after her grandmother, her mother can rest easy when she goes to work because Julia leaves the house in perfect condition, have you seen how she dresses, you'd be so much prettier if you pulled your hair back like hers, Julia's shoes are so nice, she doesn't have to wear the latest trends, why don't you make friends with Julia, it's because she hasn't been held back, you only like the girls who have to repeat, why don't you take your brother to the park like Julia does, why are you hanging around Tinker again, and that kid they call Chino, one of these days you're going to find yourself knocked up, see if you don't. And it was all true, I didn't want to hang out with Julia, I didn't want to do my hair like hers even though it looked nice and she was pretty—but I wasn't, not me—and I did like the girls who were held back or at least got bad grades, they were more fun and they made me laugh a lot more than Julia did, and it was also true that I couldn't give Silvio free rein, I had enough to handle on my own, and it was true that I had started hanging around Tinker again, I wanted to get close to his nephew—it wasn't working, not at all—and it was true that I was using Chino to boost my self-esteem and make the nephew jealous, and it was true that at just barely sixteen years old it was only a few months before I'd end up pregnant. Though I didn't know it yet, couldn't know.

But before that, the thing with Julia happened down by the canal. So many things happened in such a short time back then. Down the dark path by the canal where I would take walks with Chino—keeping him at a distance, but still hooked—hidden from everyone and hidden most of all from my aunt and uncle. A few cement benches had been put up along the path, facing the eucalyptus groves, horrible benches that broke, or got broken, and where new graffiti appeared every day. Once the weeds grew up around them, no one sat there anymore, except at night, and then it was only couples and voyeurs. This time, we were the voyeurs and they were the couple: Julia, perfect, studious Julia, sitting on an older guy's lap. Chino said he was a mechanic at the shop, that he didn't live in town. The kid had his hand up her shirt, fondling her, while she ground herself against him, threw herself on him, pressed herself to him and moved slowly up and down, rhythmically. I felt a clawing in my gut, an amalgam of bitter uneasiness, jealousy, anger, curiosity, and I wanted to sprint to my house, sprint home before I lost the urge to recount what I had seen, sprint off with no explanation, leaving Chino alone in the middle of the path. I wanted to pound on the door, wait for it to open, answer three or four of the usual questions *where have you been, why are you so late, why are you panting, you know you're late for dinner* before finding the moment, the most fitting silence among all the pauses there in the kitchen, pinpointing the instant my aunt was most relaxed while she took out the eggs, the potatoes, the bread—because despite her moods she never, ever made me go without dinner—wait for the right moment to interject, to open my mouth and begin to tell her everything I had seen, voice breaking, inexperienced with telling such stories. I wanted to continue speaking even as a look of disbelief and fury spread across my aunt's face, a paleness that warned of what I already knew was coming, but I would keep talking, nevertheless, all so that my effort, my complete, dramatic tale, would earn me no more than the most scornful of looks and a widening of her repertoire of stonewords, from that night on noticeably enriched with the addition of "rat," "wicked," "dirty-minded," "snitch," "bitter," "nasty."

But it wasn't just the stonewords. That wasn't all. There was something else, something new, an even longer expression, a full sentence, a stone sentence, one I hadn't been expecting but which she did in fact say, and which caught me off guard and hurt me for a long time, inside, deep inside, even much later when I was able to understand it.

# NOTHING NEW

HE GOT UP EARLY, not because he wasn't tired, but because he didn't feel like tossing and turning in the sweaty bed. His body ached with the pain of centuries. "Nothing new," he thought as he went downstairs to the kitchen, dragging his dry and calloused feet. "Nothing new." As soon as it saw him appear on the stairs, the cat was off like a shot into the garden, hissing in terror. The old man was completely naked and his nakedness wasn't defenseless, it was threatening: the long bones, shriveled skin, and almost translucent hair covering his back, chest, and arms, but not his thin, veiny legs. With a singular focus, he opened the refrigerator and looked for a beer. He had a raspy throat, thick tongue, and cave-like breath that he was even repulsed by. He chugged the first can without stopping for breath; then he went out into the yard with the second can to contemplate the frightened cat, bristling, poorly-hidden behind the night-blooming jasmine that, even at dawn, still stunk with hot, decaying sweetness. Beyond the fence, the sky showed its colors, liquid, drowsy, tepid with the same tepidness that at that moment ran through the old man's blood. "Nothing new," he repeated to himself, finishing the beer and stepping back into the warm house.

"Uhhh, wait a minute," Carlos said. "He wasn't in that bad of shape if he could drink a beer right out of bed."

"Oh no? Is that what you think?"

The truth was he drank at all hours of the day and hardly ate. The more he drank, the less he ate. His body was maintained solely with alcohol. He was tall and they say that as a young man he had been a good athlete; I think they're probably referring to his adolescence, given that by the time he was a young man he was already violent and lazy. He was a difficult guy. He always had been.

"The cat ran from him like he was the plague, remember?"

"It was an unsociable cat," countered Carlos. "All cats are unsociable."

"Almost all of them are. But this one was also scared of him. I saw the way he kicked it every time it crossed his path."

The cat meowed like the devil and ran from one side of the yard to the other, looking for a place to hide—it was old, like its owner, and it was hard for it to scale the wall. The old man used to kick it with his cowboy boots, and when he couldn't reach it, he would throw whatever was handy at it. That morning, behind the bushes, that cat's heart must have been racing as if it was being hunted by hounds. But the old man had watched it for barely a minute, the time it took to finish his second beer and go to the kitchen for another one. He swore out loud when he saw there weren't any left. Twenty crushed cans had accumulated on the counter, dusted with ash from the Ducados he smoked compulsively when he didn't have anything to drink. He rooted around in the cupboards until he found an almost-empty bottle of Jack Daniel's. He gulped down what was left, wiped his mouth with his forearm, and spit to the side. Then he sat on a stool, exactly as he was, naked and sweaty, his old penis flacid, head bent and supported only by one bony arm, pointy elbow digging into his knee, breathing with difficulty, and maybe without thinking about anything the whole time.

"I think he could have sat like that for hours."

"That's how my brothers and I used to find him when we visited years ago," Carlos admitted. "Naked and unwashed, until my father wouldn't let us go anymore."

"And we don't actually know if he thought about anything or not."

"Once you get to a certain age, to think about something is to think about the past, and the past is nothing, little more than nothing."

"I'm not so sure."

He used to repeat his old refrain "nothing new, nothing new." And yet he maintained his look of calm astonishment in crusty eyes open wide, that strange, defeated curiosity that leads one to look around without really being surprised by anything. He sat naked in the kitchen for hours, on a morning in August but also in February, when the frigid air seeped in through the windows and the floor frosted over from the cold. He was tough and he never got sick. We never saw him cough, he never went to the doctor.

"He bragged about that, didn't he?"

"About what?" Carlos had stopped listening and was

leaning indolently against the wall with the same abandon with which his grandfather spent hours and hours on a stool in the kitchen.

"That he had never been to a doctor. For him it was a point of pride."

"Yeah, it was. He never went to see the doctor. Not even on the day of his death was he examined by a doctor. All they did was record the minutes of what had happened." Carlos paused a moment and then lowered his voice to continue. "But I wasn't there. That's what I was told."

Nevertheless, that day was the same as the other days in that he got up early, drank, and sat on the kitchen stool thinking about nothing. Spreading his skinny hairless legs, penis falling over swollen testicles, breath ragged with anger, and those watery, astonished eyes, he waited for time to pass until he could go out and buy more beer and more whiskey. The sun had just fully risen and the sky had lost its shades of liquid pink, but there were still two hours until the stores would open, and those two hours had to be spent right there, beside the kitchen door, while his cat stayed out in the yard, crouched, motionless, except for its twitching tail. And maybe he would contemplate—without seeing them—the plants charred by the August sun, resentful of the lack of watering—by that time nobody went around to see him or help him with chores around the house—and the flower bed where blackbirds had stirred up the soil pecking for worms.

"There was a woman who did go to help him. A Polish woman my mother found. He paid her miserably, when he paid her at all. She could have left him rotting there but she felt pity for him and kept going one day a week to do a little laundry and fix him a hot meal."

"I heard the house was a disaster."

"It probably was," Carlos admitted. "One day a week wasn't enough. My grandfather spent the whole day shut up in there and didn't care about anything. He never cared about cleaning. At the end, he liked destroying whatever he found around him."

"So you don't have a very good opinion of him either."

"It isn't an opinion, it's a fact. And it's the same reason I tell you that he didn't drink right out of bed and that his cat wasn't afraid of him. Saying that isn't defending him. It's simply saying how things really were."

But the old man was still sitting there after emptying two cans of beer and a quarter of a bottle of whiskey, the same way the cat was still there crouching and afraid, and not even the old man's grandson Carlos—who hadn't seen him in years—could claim that was untrue. And when the doctor arrived and certified his death, he also saw all the crushed cans covered in ash on the counter, but he couldn't know that on that August morning—his last morning—he had let the hours go by, seated on the kitchen stool, muttering his old litany of "nothing new, nothing new." Nor that the hours had gone by slowly, and when it was nine o'clock, or a little after nine, when the old man had gotten up to go for more provisions, the bell had rung at the dilapidated old house, and it was the postwoman delivering some threatening certified letters having to do with unpaid bills.

"I'm not sure about that, either."

"You mean about the bills?"

"No, not about the bills. About the doorbell ringing. About that woman even going to the house. But go on," Carlos said.

He opened the door, naked, and the postwoman, who was new in the neighborhood and had never delivered anything to that house, wasn't surprised. She looked him up and down calmly, without getting scared or laughing—not even to herself—and held out the certified letters for him to sign. Something odd must have passed through the old man's head, because he invited her in.

"And she says he did," Carlos whispered.

"Yes. They say she had a premonition. She thought something strange was happening inside that house and that she had to see it, whatever it was. And the fact that that man, that stranger, was naked and stank of alcohol didn't stop her."

"My grandfather was a skinny old guy with no strength left. There was no reason to be afraid of him."

"Yeah, but there was violence in his eyes. And any woman would be scared of a naked man, regardless of how old he was, while if it were the opposite, a man would feel pity or disgust."

"You can't be sure she wasn't disgusted."

"No, I can't be sure."

Because she was an attractive young woman—a little common, maybe, according to some, but attractive in any case—and although she entered the little house with barely a thought, she still couldn't be considered a shameless woman, nor that she was motivated by anything other than innocent, unnuanced curiosity. The old man, who had probably forgotten that he was naked, looked at her straight on and offered her coffee. Maybe she told him that she couldn't stay long, and he assured her it would only be a couple of minutes. She looked for the coffee maker herself among the dirty pots and pans piled in the sink; she washed it and added the water and the coffee and put it on the small, blackened stove. And that was when the old man—who had sat back down on the stool, though now with his chin jutted and haughty—introduced himself and asked just who she was exactly and why she had come to visit him so early in the morning.

"Obviously, he had mixed things up and didn't even realize that the woman was the postwoman, he thought she'd just rang his doorbell to hand him some threatening notifications regarding unpaid bills or whatever; in truth that doesn't really matter."

"No, that isn't the important thing," Carlos repeated.

"They say the woman reminded him of someone."

"She must have. Otherwise there's no explanation for inviting her in."

"He could have asked anybody inside. It's possible she was the only person who rang the doorbell that day."

"We can't be sure of that, either. Maybe someone rang but left unnoticed."

And the old man observed her, he observed the woman beyond space and time, seated on his stool, in the grimy, inhospitable kitchen, while she made coffee and looked sideways at all the crushed beer cans and empty bottles, without saying a word, without asking any questions. Then the woman poured the coffee in two cups she just finished washing and put one next to the old man, and they drank in silence, as if right then everything was normal."

"The woman shouldn't have gone in. She had some nerve," Carlos said.

"You said yourself before that your grandfather couldn't have scared anybody, not even his cat, not even a woman, not even when he was naked from head to foot."

"It's possible. But she shouldn't have gone in. She was motivated by morbid curiosity. He smelled like death and she wanted to see it close up. She wanted to look death square in the eyes. Spur it on, maybe."

"And yet, he said something to her. Something revelatory, even if you don't like it."

"I'm not really sure about that. She could have made it up. She could have heard rumors about him somewhere else, and showed up at his house later, giving herself a starring role in my grandfather's final hours, being the one who got him to talk about memories he had buried long ago."

"Why would she do that?"

"To be in your story."

And that was why one day, not too near in the future but not too far off, either, Carlos would have to confront her and find out if it was true that she had conversed with the old man or if, on the contrary, they had simply sipped their coffee in silence, or if she'd downed hers, stood up, grabbed her little cart on wheels, and left, off to finish delivering the mail on the street with the old houses flanked by depressing magnolias and jasmine bushes, or if she had, in fact, never actually been inside the house, never saw the crushed cans, and all she had done was repeat what she'd heard other people say, the Polish cleaning lady, maybe. But if they had talked—if it was true, the story she told afterward—then first the old man had started to whisper a series of commands, commands related to lines and hands, and then he raised his voice and his mild tone became shouting and he lifted his hand as if to smack her across the face—the skinny right arm held aloft, tendons strained in rage—and first he called her "Red" and then "whore" and then "Red whore" and muttered obscenities, while his eyes looked backward, back to another time of shame and fury. And according to what the woman would later claim to anyone who would listen, there was zero remorse in his voice, zero remorse, but there was dark, festering hatred that could no longer be transformed into action, impotent now and not for lack of will, but because of age, just like the old man had to get up every day not for lack of tiredness, but because of the burning sheets, or had to stop drinking not for lack of thirst, but lack of drink. And the woman felt a mix of compassion and disgust—yes, disgust—for the old Francoist colonel, and stood up after she'd confirmed that he had signed the receipt of the certified unpaid bills, and suppressing the bitterness of the woman she was inside and whoever the woman the old madman was addressing had been, thanked him for the coffee and perhaps, fully aware that she was silencing the voice of all violated women, even shook his hand.

"And he didn't even try to go get more booze afterward," Carlos continued, accepting, for the first time, that all the above could be true.

He didn't go out for more booze. For a few more hours he sat on the kitchen stool—maybe he nodded off, maybe the cat took its chance to come inside and shelter under the stairs—until gradually, bit by bit, the hour of his death arrived.

"A peaceful death, a gentle one; a death he maybe didn't deserve," Carlos admitted.

And the woman—that woman new to the neighborhood, young and attractive and a little common all at once—later told her version, what it had seemed like to her, and reiterated that there had been no remorse in the old man's words, though one had to admit that *she* was a little brazen—what kind of woman accepts an invitation inside from a naked man, even if that man is over eighty?—and brazen women tend to lie, and maybe she had already heard things from some of neighbor women, maybe nothing happened to her after all, maybe, like Carlos says, she didn't really have coffee with the old man, maybe she didn't even knock on his door, because maybe the unpaid bills didn't exist, and if they did, it's not like they would have been paper notices that some insignificant and anonymous postwoman could have handed over directly in person.

# WHITE PEOPLE

IT WAS THREATENING TO snow, but inside the heat made
the windows so foggy that I didn't see him until he came in
and stood right in front of me with his attitude of a man
who knows what he's doing and doesn't care about anything,
or anybody, but himself. Mario, his name was. I had been
waiting for him for almost an hour, sitting there, not knowing
what else to order, while the waitress from Bolivia or Ecuador
or one of those places circled my table like she was sussing
me out. Mario and Mariola: it was like a bad joke. Waiting
for him for almost an hour and I didn't even have the guts
to call him out. It was because of how he looked. I hadn't
imagined him like that, even though I'm not really sure what I
had imagined. He was a dark guy, thin, with a teeny-tiny ring
in his ear. He came in his work coverall and hiking boots. His
hands were grease stained. He looked bad and he smelled bad.
He took out a pack of smokes and lit a cigarette. He didn't
offer me one. He sat down across from me, spread his arms on
the table and watched me for a few seconds before he spoke.
I remember that my teeth started to chatter.

"Tell me what really happened," he said point blank.

"You don't believe what Mariola told you?

He laughed. He had a few chipped teeth.

"Mariola? Mariola's a liar. You can't trust what she tells you."

"Well, look," I whispered. "It's all exactly like she says."


You have to come, she'd begged. Fine, I thought. A nice opportunity to escape the family notions shop and see a bit of the world and all that. My parents would be mad, no avoiding that. But I had the right to visit my sister every once in a while. When someone in the family needs help, you show up, that's what I'd always been taught. The problem was, I couldn't tell them exactly what kind of help. Mariola insisted that I couldn't tell anybody anything. Just come and forget about the rest, she said, as if it was that easy. She seemed so worried about her own situation that she had forgotten how different things are here. She's never stopped to think about what my life is like since she decided to move to Cárdenas, what she left me to deal with on my own. So when she called and asked me to come, I felt a mix of joy and dread. Joy because I was excited to pack my suitcase; dread because I didn't know how to work it out so they wouldn't complain too much. I'd have to lie. Again.

"Mariola can't come home for Christmas Eve. She invited me to spend a few days with her before."

My mother took a short pause, an elastic band laced between her swollen fingers. She asked me how many days we were talking about.

"Three or four."

"Don't forget that you'll be leaving us alone here at the shop."

"I haven't seen Mariola in a long time."

"She should come here."

"She can't, mamá, I just told you. Because of work."

"And your job? Your job doesn't matter?"

"It'll just be two or three days."

Actually, it all depended on when the birth would happen, but I couldn't tell her that either. There are too many things I can't tell her, not her, not my father. Not bad things, but still, things they wouldn't understand, and I have to hide or cover them up to avoid problems. They hardly ever asked Mariola to explain herself. She never told us exactly what she did or stopped doing, where she lived or with whom. My sister—the bright one, the college graduate, the daughter who went to work in Cárdenas, who condemned me to stay here and help—had free rein to do whatever she wanted: call or stop calling, come or stop coming, they didn't give her a hard time, no matter what she did. She was the pride of my parents, who—while they lectured me for coming home a few minutes late—didn't even know she was forty weeks pregnant.


From the train, I watch the scenery slip past, the dry, frozen plateau in December, the fields; a dull landscape but different, at least, from the one I saw day after day. Nevertheless, the feeling it produced was identical to the one that ravaged me when I feasted my eyes on the village: the low brick houses, the old men sitting in the plaza, the lame dogs, the farms in the distance: the same flat, shallow horizon, the same fatigue.

I arrived in Cárdenas at a decent hour, but I preferred to wait and let Mariola know the next day. I absolutely didn't want her thinking that I couldn't take care of myself. Beside the station, I saw rows and rows of cabs that people hailed without forming any sort of line. I considered taking one, then thought how I couldn't be wasting money like that. I ruled out the metro, too, because I was afraid of getting lost among so many lines—blue, red, gray, green—intersecting over and over. With the address in hand and pausing to use the maps at the bus stops along the way, I walked some eight or ten kilometers until I found the street I was looking for. The hostel occupied the shabby, damp ground floor of an old building. The room was simple, just like Mariola had said. It cost thirty euros a night. The bedspread smelled like cheap detergent, the floor smelled like bleach, and the sink was rust stained. The bathtub and toilet were located in a cramped hovel at the end of the hall, and were shared between three or four other rooms. Mariola assured me that you couldn't get anything better for that price. I thought it was fine, but I imagined what my parents would say if they could see me there. Maybe they thought Mariola was living in a luxury penthouse or modern studio downtown, when the truth was that she didn't even have a bed for me.

I hardly slept that first night. My window faced the back of some dive, a cocktail lounge that had the look of a gambling den. All night I had to listen to employees coming and going, hauling out trash, shouting the whole time, even a fight between two—I think—Chinese people who shrieked as if they were stabbing each other. I was anxious and too tired to sleep. I set the alarm for eight, but it hadn't been necessary. By seven-thirty, the sun was up and I was already dressed and half-way outside when the hostel's manager, a big, light-skinned Black woman—a *mulatta*, that was the word—stopped me in the doorway.

"You gotta pay before you go."

"I'll be back later," I promised. "I'm not leaving yet. I'll be back later."

"You gotta pay before you go. You pay after every night."

The manager was like that, blunt. The night before, she had already told me—in accented Spanish—that I couldn't have guests in my room—"bring a muchacho and the rate is double"—and if I wanted the room cleaned or needed fresh towels I had to pay an extra five euros a night—"and I gotta know before ten." She studied me so fixedly with her blood-shot, chocolatey eyes that I had no choice but to submit. I grudgingly took out the money and handed it over without meeting her eye. She inspected the bills and tucked them into one of the pockets of her housecoat, nodding for me to get out of her sight once and for all.

I had breakfast at VIPS. It was too pricey for my bud-get, but also anonymous enough, and I didn't feel like being noticed. Even so, the girl waiting on me looked me up and down, as if wondering where I'd come from. I wolfed down my toast, protecting myself behind a newspaper someone had left on the table. From the corner of my eye, I studied the other girls eating by themselves. They looked independent, sure of themselves, powerful, and a little manly. They were all wearing slouchy leather boots with a bow at the back, no heel. Comparing their boots to mine, uneasiness took root in the pit of my stomach. I called Mariola when I finished breakfast. She told me she'd just gotten up; she felt heavy and a little dizzy; her man had gone to work and wouldn't be back until the evening; she had plans to meet the *other* guy at twelve-thirty; she and I could meet at eleven, in front of the hostel. I still had more than two hours to kill.

I walked down the whole length of Calle Central and then turned into the area around Casielles. It was intensely cold, cutting. I liked the decorations in the streets, the Christmas lights—off at that time of day—the striking Christmas displays in the storefronts full of—among other things—slouchy leather boots with bows in the back, all way more expensive than what I could afford. A tide of people swelled from one side of the street to the other, not looking at each other, and not looking at me. On every street corner there were a dozen guys wearing signs around their necks: WE BUY & SELL GOLD. A few Romanian guys, very dark-skinned, with their gold molars, rubbed their gloved hands together and murmured among themselves in their strange language. I liked everything, even that.

I passed City Hall, the San Lázaro market, and the Lateral. Later, when the stores opened, I went back for some tights I'd seen in a notions shop, an establishment that wasn't called a "notions shop" likes ours was, but Fabrics and Threads, which sounded much better. I spent four euros on the tights. They were very cool, with green and purple diamond shapes and lace at the heel and toe. We would've never sold them in our store, not only because we didn't receive items like that, but because we wouldn't have had anyone to sell them to. The salesgirls were starting to pull the light-up Santas and signs with tinsel and pom-poms out to the sidewalk. I felt euphoric.

It was impossible to imagine what would happen just a few hours later. Remembering that walk—the streets I strolled, the storefronts I stopped at, the decorations I watched get put out and turned on, the crowds, the tights—is proof that the world maintains a steady pulse, even when it all seems to be accelerating. Faced with whatever happens, the world is impassive, no matter how unusual, horrible, or cruel it may be. The world, from this perspective, doesn't really have much to do with us at all.

*Like a gnawed pomegranate.* A head, split open like a gnawed pomegranate. That was the image that came to my mind in the moment, and the one that would keep coming later, projected over and over on my brain. I remembered the bleeding head— bleeding just like pomegranate pips—and I looked at Mario who was smoking and staring at the foggy window, impatient, violent, distracted. Wordlessly, he scratched his arms. Then his expression changed and he laughed. A madman's laugh.

"Shit, Mariola's so skinny, that must've taken a lotta balls."

I didn't reply. I didn't know what to say. The waitress came to take our order and we asked for a couple of Cokes. Mario was still laughing to himself, laughing through closed teeth, as if conscientiously chewing his own laughter.

"What I don't understand is why she changed her mind," he said.

There was a strange glint in his eyes.

"We talked about it. We didn't want the baby."

"She does now."

"Fuck what she wants! She wants to screw me over, that's what."

I don't know whether or not she wanted to screw him over. Enough time had passed so I don't know Mariola anymore; I don't know what her reasons could be for acting the way she acts, I don't know what her desires or interests or ends are or anything. It's been too many years since we really talked. There's always a barrier between us, a kind of translucent wall through which we see the disfigured image of the other. I even had trouble recognizing her when I first saw her. Not because of the enormous belly under her coat—I had been expecting that—but because she now had a pixie-style haircut, longish tufts left to cover her ears, because she was pale and her cheekbones were sharp. She was wearing a tracksuit and sneakers and looked like a sick person. She smiled with white, chapped lips and we hugged clumsily right there.

Mariola had always been sinewy, strong, thin, as if carefully molded. The tight, pointy belly didn't seem to belong to her. Seeing it—the belly—made me feel more disgust than tenderness; it was like a big chunk of meat tacked onto her waist, a heavy sash, foreign and problematic. We walked for several minutes, not looking at each other or speaking, and then we went to have a coffee at a bar farther down the street, a typical bar I would've never gone in alone, with its glass countertop and paneled walls and idle fifty-somethings drinking anisettes with the collars of their jackets turned up. Mariola looked at me with disinterest. She didn't even ask if I'd had an okay trip or how my night had been. She got right to the point. She examined the palms of her hands, then looked up and said:

"I changed my mind. I'm keeping the baby."

The waiter turned to watch us. I stuttered:

"But what will happen now? That guy is coming at twelve-thirty, right?"

"Yeah, he's coming to the apartment. I'll tell him then."

"He has no idea?"

"No, he has no idea yet."

There was a pause. Even the other patrons seemed to go still. The noise in the bar was suspended, stalled, more inconvenient than ominous.

"Does he know?"

"I just told you no! Are you stupid?"

Mariola was famously bad-tempered.

"I mean your boyfriend, Mario. What does he have to say?"

"Nothing. He doesn't know either. I decided last night, by myself."

She grabbed her cup and sipped her coffee, eyes down. As for me, I didn't dare say anything else.


I was surprised by the hovel they lived in. In comparison, my room at the hostel was almost luxurious. Their place was in a building shored up with scaffolding, one of those crumbling apartment buildings full of old people and immigrants, with peeling walls and a stairwell railing sticky with built-up grease. My sister and Mario rented the top floor, where the elevator didn't even reach and there was no automatic buzzer. It was probably a storage room in other times. There was a single, tiny window that barely let in any light and a kind of closet with a sink, toilet, and a small square shower tray. The bed, folding table, and wardrobe barely fit in the bedroom. I had to sit on the bed to wait. My sister lay down beside me, staring at the ceiling. I thought about my mother, about what she would have said if she knew that her daughter, the bright one, the college grad, was living in such a slum. At the time, I still would have given anything to change places with her. At least she was free, even if her freedom consisted of living there. I watched her out of the corner of my eye, her enormous belly rising and falling from her breath—or from nervousness—listening to the tick-tock of an old, rusted alarm clock.

At twelve-thirty, with alarming punctuality, someone knocked on the door. My sister got up and murmured something I couldn't make out. Then she opened the door and he came in, smiling, his white, affable hand outstretched.

"Hi. I'm José de la Cruz."

I didn't like his smile one bit. Actually I didn't like anything about him. His attitude was sure and sporting; the way he waltzed in and stood there seemed to suggest that he expected everyone to turn toward him, as if admiring him were the natural thing to do. He was tall, strong, tanned and well-dressed, a pair of blue, pleated trousers and a sport coat still giving off the heat of an iron. He gave Mariola's hand a soft shake and then looked at me questioningly.

"This is my sister," Mariola said. "She's here with me."

"Good, of course, no problem."

He weighed me with a glance, as if measuring me. Then he swapped his composure for a more urgent, intimate tone.

"Look, Mariola, I wanted to meet you before . . . before . . . well you know. I know it isn't orthodox, but, basically, I wanted to thank you."

Mariola looked at him coldly and scowled. When she showed her disgust, her lips stretched so thin they disappeared. I knew that expression extremely well, I knew the danger in it, but the man did not. He hurried on.

"I thought you might need some money. Now, they couldn't find out about that. There's no reason to tell anybody what we do, our private agreements. There's nothing wrong with it, you know? Nothing wrong."

He rubbed his clean-shaven cheeks and his eyebrows rose a little higher.

"There's no problem on our part. What we want, you know, what we want is for everything to go well. To help with whatever you ask for, so it all goes well."

"That will no longer be necessary," Mariola replied slowly, biting off every syllable. "I'm keeping the baby."

The man tensed. First, he opened his mouth soundlessly, then his cheeks and forehead flushed.

"What?" he whispered.

Mariola sat back down on the bed, opening her legs wide to accommodate her belly. She explained that she had changed her mind, that was all. She had the right, she said twice; she had the right.

"But you can't do that!"

The situation was suddenly out of his control.

Mariola took a cigarette from the nightstand and lit it with provocative calm. Of course she could, she said. She was.

"You must be kidding. You're trying to scare me, right?"

"No, I'm serious."

The man took a few steps in her direction. I saw his hands shaking. His Adam's apple bobbed up and down, like he was swallowing. His shout came after he moved toward her, not at the same time. That I do remember clearly, it was *after*, and his voice sharpened, became high-pitched, unmasculine.

"What am I going to tell my wife now? Have you thought about how I'll explain this to her?"

Mariola looked at him impassively. She took another drag from the cigarette and held his gaze. She seemed fairly calm. In contrast, his trembling was becoming increasingly intense. Through the little window, a ray of light shone square on his face, emphasizing his already unhinged features.

"You'll never be a good mother! Get it? Never! Where will you raise your son? In this shithole? In this dump a beggar on the street wouldn't want? Are you crazy? Do you want more money? What the fuck is wrong with you?"

"There's nothing wrong with me. I just changed my mind."

"You just changed your mind," he repeated. He moved in on her. "There's no word for girls like you. You can't be trusted, none of you."

I sat stock-still. I don't like shouting and I don't like when the neighbors can overhear. I believe in discussing things calmly, without yelling. But I didn't feel threatened. I thought the guy would holler some more, try to convince Mariola, then leave. I wasn't even that offended by his attack—"none of you." Inwardly, I hoped Mariola would change her mind again, that everything would go back to the way it was before. I think that's when he grabbed her arm. He probably didn't hurt her, but she screeched like a rat.

"Let go of me!"

He didn't let go. He started insulting her. He held her loosely by the arm, but his insults were vicious. He called her a whore and things like that. I remember that, as he spoke, he seemed to calm down, his body going slack, legs apart, swaying in rage and despair. Then I saw my sister clutch the old alarm clock, I saw her raise her arm and I saw streak of rust, I saw the metal bash into his forehead, and I saw his eyes look at me, bewildered. He took a step back, stumbled against my legs, and tumbled backward onto me. I recoiled and he fell all the way. As he fell he turned as if looking for something, and his temple rushed toward the edge of the folding table, or the folding table rushed toward his temple, and his head cracked like a gnawed pomegranate, a dark red and grainy gash. I jumped back. I don't think I could even scream.

I never imagined it would be so easy to kill a man.

The strangest part of it is, the wound I saw didn't exist. The blow itself was enough: a clean blow, regrettably well-aimed. What I saw was something else, a kind of hallucination. I saw, perhaps, what lay beyond the blow: the effect of a bite taken out of a man's life, the fragility of a man's life. I blinked and looked again. He had an odd grimace on his parted lips, a frozen stare. There was no blood.

My sister and I were shocked, but not terribly afraid at first. I ran to her and looked at her closely, my forehead against hers. It was self-defense, we told ourselves; it was self-defense, he had tried to strangle her. After that, there was no other explanation to give.

What came next is so hazy that it's hard to put the events in order. The first thing I see—the first thing I remember—is being in a claustrophobic room at the police station, giving my statement to a pair of too-friendly cops. Other things must have happened before then, yet all I have are foggy, diluted images that I can't quite bring into focus, like in dreams: neighbors gathered in the doorway, the ambulance and its whirring lights, Mariola walking down the stairs, supporting her belly, the police van and the two of us sitting together, not a word between us.

"How did José de la Cruz attempt to attack your sister?"

The cop squinted. It wasn't that he was particularly interested in the question, but a nervous tic, one he repeated every few seconds.

"He wanted to strangle her."

*He held Mariola's arm loosely, as he insulted her slowly, meticulously, unhurried. I stayed on the sidelines, watching his pupils dilate like marbles, he looked right at me the moment he fell.*

"Can you explain what happened in more detail?"

"No. It happened so fast. I can't really remember."

"You must remember something."

"Not much, really."

"It's best if you try."

His voice was threatening. *The gnawed pomegranate.* I swallowed.

"He came at Mariola really angry, calling her names. He tried to grab her by the throat. That's all I remember."

"He tried to grab her, or he grabbed her?"

"He grabbed her."

The cop looked over some papers a clerk brought in; he looked at them blankly, killing time. It seemed like he didn't really know where to start. He sighed and observed me again through squinted eyes. The other cop—stronger, handsomer—kept quiet.

"When he arrived at the apartment, was Mr. de la Cruz aggressive? Was he behaving violently from the start?"

"No. At first he was calm, really happy. But then he got really upset when Mariola told him she'd changed her mind."

"Why did she wait to the last minute to tell him?"

"I don't know. I'd just found out myself."

There was a brief silence. I could hear a distant noise that put me on edge, a rhythmic sound from an unknown source. The cop continued his questioning.

"Where did your sister meet José de la Cruz?"

"I'm not really sure. Mariola is anti-abortion; she's very religious. Maybe she got in touch with him through her church. Or through an adoption agency. All I know is that it was totally legal."

"Yes, we know that already. But it's odd that your sister would ask him to meet her at home. Do you know why she did that?"

"I guess to tell him that she changed her mind."

"I think it was for something else."

He coughed and leaned in close.

"She didn't say anything about changing her mind on the phone. Hadn't they discussed money? Weren't they meeting about money?"

"No."

"Are you sure?"

"Yes."

He sighed and examined his fingernails. The other cop must have found this amusing because he was smiling to himself. The clicking noise continued, pitapat, *and there was the gnawed pomegranate, splitting open a little deeper, weeping black and red seeds, and Mariola didn't seem to grasp that she'd just killed a man.*

"We also know that Mr. De la Cruz was a pleasant guy. Easy, low-key. Not the profile of a violent person who'd let himself get carried away by anger or attempt to murder somebody who contradicted him."

"Well, I can assure you that he was very angry."

"To the point of wanting to strangle a pregnant woman?"

The cop reviewed a document that had the look of a medical report. He squinted again.

"He took a serious blow. A person who's being strangled doesn't have the strength to drive an alarm clock into somebody's forehead. Are you sure your sister acted in self-defense?"

"Of course I'm sure. Besides, he didn't die from the alarm clock. He died when he fell, when he hit his temple. It was an accident."

"Are you a pathologist?"

"No."

"Then be quiet and stick to answering the questions you're asked. Tell me, for example, why your sister doesn't have marks on her neck. Not even a tiny scrape, not a scratch, not a bruise, nothing."

"I don't know."

*José de la Cruz's slack arm, and my sister's, sinewy and aloft.*

"I don't want to talk anymore."

I'd seen in the movies that if you didn't want to continue, you could refuse to answer.

The cop stood. Pensive, he shuffled the papers on the table. I stayed in the metal chair, hands crossed on my knees, a little shaky and very hungry. The short cop looked at the better-looking one, turned down the corners of his mouth, and, shrugging, made to go to the door. Then he turned back.

"One last question. If she was being attacked like that, why didn't you do something to defend your sister?"

I didn't reply. I just wanted to get out of there, forget everything. None of it was my problem.


Mariola was brought to the maternity ward at Santa Catalina hospital. She was under police supervision, but a medical exam had determined that she could go into labor at any moment and needed to be admitted. Her apartment was cordoned off with police tape. They said it didn't even meet hygienic standards for habitation. They let me go, under conditions, or something like that. I asked what it meant.

"You have to come sign in at the station every morning. You must be available to come any time you're called. And you can't leave the city."

"For how long?"

"For as long as necessary."

I didn't understand what warranted such close supervision. I had nothing to do with any of it; I just had the bad luck of being there, of being a direct witness to an ugly situation. It wasn't my problem, I told myself repeatedly, it wasn't my problem. Mariola had been clear that I wasn't guilty of anything. She admitted to being the sole perpetrator of the crime—"the sole perpetrator," all the terminology made me feel like I was living in a movie—but she continued to insist that she had acted in self-defense.

I wasn't allowed to see her for the first three days. I stayed alone in Cárdenas, in the cheap hostel, not really knowing what to do with myself. I called my parents and relayed that I would be gone a little longer. Mariola, I said, was excited for me to spend Christmas Eve with her.

"And what about us?" my mother shouted. "Are we just supposed to go along with whatever you want? Why don't you both come here? You've been gone long enough, spending money, don't you think? Between the shop and the house, there are a thousand things that need doing around here and I can't do it all! I need a rest, too!"

I could hear my father grumbling in the background.

They were really angry, but there was nothing I could do. I had no idea when I would be allowed to leave. I had to stay there as long as necessary, isn't that what they'd said? But how long was necessary? At the moment, I was more worried about the grief I was going get at home than how the whole Cárdenas mess was going to be resolved. Everything led to a serious telling-off. And if I stopped to think about it—The Serious Telling-Off—was more disturbing to me than anything else in the world.

I met Mario later. He came to the hostel while I was out. The busty mulatta told me when I got back after one of my mornings out window-shopping, the only thing I could do for free to pass the time.

"He left this number for you to call him," she said. "And another thing. When are you leaving? Prices go up on Christmas Eve. I told you that the first day."

The woman's nearness made me uncomfortable. She was impossible to avoid, always lurking at the bottom of the staircase. By the way she looked at me, one eyebrow raised and a grimace of disgust, I got the sense that she knew everything that had happened and had already formed her own opinion on the subject.

I grabbed the piece of paper with the number on it and thanked her, hiding the sandwich I was bringing back to my room under my coat. We weren't allowed to eat in the rooms, but I couldn't be fooling around with my money. Eating out was becoming prohibitive.

Still, I arranged to meet Mario at VIPS. I couldn't think of anywhere better. And it was silly, because the meeting was pointless. With his stupid little earring and his greasy, grimy look, the workman's coverall and his way of smoking and watching me, he repeated that Mariola was a fraud and all she wanted was to screw him over.

"To screw me, that's all she's wanted from the start."

Then he told me that the police had called him, as well, and asked him a few things. They were very considerate with him, he said, they listened to him carefully and believed everything he said.

"The truth comes first, I've always said. Not like Mariola, always hiding things, always scheming, always two-faced. I couldn't care less about what either of you have to say now."

"Then why did you want to see me?" I interrupted. "What do you want?"

"I want to know if your family will help."

For the first time, he smiled. A twisted, ugly smile with dirty, gapped teeth.

"Help with what?"

"Don't play dumb. Are you going to help with the baby? A baby needs money and I don't have it. The family has a responsibility, too. Family is there to lend a hand. Mariola never talks about any of you, but I think it's time for things to change around here."

"Yeah, it's time for things to change," I whispered.

"So?"

I told him that yes, we would help however we could, although I thought of my parents and how it would be better if they never found out they were going to have a grandson. I wished with all my might that I could go back in time and make things how they'd always been, even if that condemned us all to an eternal life among the rice fields.

We left. Mario watched me mockingly as I paid for the two Cokes. He grunted goodbye and walked out, buttoning his jacket up to his chin. To live in Cárdenas and end up with a guy like that, I thought with fake pity. An erratic semi-snow was falling, so I went into El Corte Inglés to try on clothes. I didn't know what else to do.

I got a really good deal on the boots. Slouchy, synthetic leather boots, flat with a bow at the back, for just twenty euros. A Christmas special. I spent the whole day walking around in them. In my jeans, hat, and boots, pacing the streets I now knew like the back of my hand, I started to feel like I was finally a part of Cárdenas, and, for a little while, forgot everything else. Then I got a call from the police and went to see Mariola at the hospital. The baby had been born the night before. Maybe I wanted to see him, they suggested: visits from relatives were allowed. It was the 23rd and there was something in the air, what some people call Christmas spirit. The streets were filled with Santa Clauses handing out candy and balloons and people in red hats just because, leafleteers dressed as Wisemen handing out flyers, carolers accompanied by tambourines and panhandlers asking for change as they wished you a Merry Christmas.

As I was about to enter the hospital, my father called to ask what was going on.

"Don't tell me you aren't coming home for Christmas Eve with your family."

His voice sounded metallic, different. It was strange, him talking. He never asked questions. He restricted himself to stating his point of view and backing you into a corner if you tried to refute it.

"Mariola is also my family. Besides, there are no tickets left."

"That's a lie. I called the train station and was told that there are."

"I'm sorry, Papá. I have to stay a few more days."

I faltered and decided to play my last card.

"I'll explain everything when I get home."

"You just don't want to come back. You love a good party and there's plenty of that in Cárdenas."

"No, Papá, that's not it at all. I'll explain everything later."

"I'm telling you right now that if you don't come home, your mother and I are going to show up there."

I wanted to believe he was bluffing. I had to believe it was a bluff, that he wasn't being serious, couldn't be serious. I felt my hands go cold, stiff, as I stood at the hospital entrance.

"I'll call you, Papá. My phone's almost dead."

I was a bundle of nerves as I went inside. I found Mariola in a regular room, a room all to herself. I don't know why I'd imagined that she'd been under guard or handcuffed or whatever. Truth is, I got to her without anybody asking a single question. Mariola was sleeping with the baby beside her in a little swivel crib. His eyes were open and his mouth milk-stained. He had a ton of hair and was horrifically small and ugly. I took his hand and he gripped me with his teeny-tiny fingers. His fingernails were long and soft and his wrinkly skin was covered with golden fuzz. He looked at me with murky eyes and mewed a little. Mariola woke up.

We didn't talk about any of it. I mean, nothing related to José de la Cruz or her arrest or my situation or hers. She seemed really tired. She told me it had been a long labor, the baby hadn't wanted to come out and she hadn't slept the whole night because he hadn't stopped crying, not for even a minute.

"What's his name?"

"I don't know yet."

She sat up a little to look at him. She was pale and her hair was messy. Suddenly, she looked like a sick little girl.

The baby fussed and she picked him up and brought him to her breast. Her nipple was like a purple plum; I never could have imagined my sister with such a big nipple. I stared, fascinated, for a few seconds.

Then Mario came and I had to go.


If anything bothered me, it was the thought of the woman at the hostel imagining the worst about me. The looks she gave me were getting more sinister. She was always around, in her pinny and the floral dresses that barely covered her blazing breasts. It was pointless to try and avoid her since she insisted I pay for each night separately. The evening of the 24th, I snuck out like a criminal to go get something to eat. The sun had already set, it was fairly cold, and the few people still out were walking like they were in a big hurry. I had trouble finding an open shop. I finally went into a Chinese bodega and bought a couple of sandwiches, two yogurts, and a carton of juice. Halfway to the hostel, I turned back around and bought a package of palmier pastries for breakfast the next morning.

I wasn't the only one who spent Christmas Eve in the hostel. From seven till nine, my neighbor—an old guy with a stutter, a Pole, I think—turned on his radio and listened to the same soul music program like he did every night. The couple at the end of the hall made a bit of a racket, nothing out of the ordinary really: they sang Christmas carols and later had a fight. As for the manager, she mucked about in the hallway the whole time. I heard her shouting on the phone and the clatter of the bucket being set on the floor as she cleaned. I smelled disinfectant all night.

I called Mariola but her cellphone was disconnected. I sent the same Merry Christmas message to a couple of girlfriends. Only one wrote back. I almost missed my parents. Inside my room at the hostel, the hours dragged by; a TV would have been nice. At eight-thirty, I ate dinner in bed, flipping through a magazine I'd taken from the hospital the day before. Then I dozed off until about midnight, when I heard fireworks and cars passing and the night began to liven up. I looked out the window and saw that a line of girls in miniskirts and platform heels and guys in leather jackets was forming behind the dive bar. The girls had no problem getting in, but the guys were stopped by two beefy dudes with wide stances, their arms crossed over their chests. I don't know why people were going in through the back door and not the front that night. They were there until five or six in the morning, when I sensed the commotion start to die down. Finally, I fell asleep.

They'd excused me from sign-in at the police station on Christmas Day. I spent the morning in the hostel, sleeping on and off and being bored. I finished off the palmiers. In the afternoon, I went out for a few hours to visit Mariola and her nameless baby. I took advantage of the fact that we were together and called our parents, thinking it would help calm them down. They still seemed pretty mad, but not at her. I watched Mariola chat with them. She was animated, smiling, and giving vague answers. I imagined that was enough for them, and I bristled with envy. When they asked whose baby was crying, she lied with startling ease:

"Oh, we're visiting a neighbor who just had a baby."

Mariola proved oddly relaxed. Her breath was even and the circles under her eyes had disappeared almost completely. She told me that she and Mario had argued that morning. He was still set on giving up the baby for adoption, while she was increasingly sure she wanted to keep him, despite the fact that she was obviously detached from the newborn and still hadn't even named him. She also told me that she would be released from the hospital the next day, and from there, be sent to a women's prison.

"It's pre-trial detention. It doesn't mean anything yet. It's because I can't stay at home, not like this. Otherwise, house arrest would be fine. That's pretty much what they told me."

"What about the baby?"

"The baby will come with me. We'll be fine there."

On my way back to the hostel, I went around to the front of the dive bar. The place was called the Oasis and it was a kind of lounge that was open, according to the sign, from 4 P.M. to 1 A.M. in the morning, though I was well-aware that they closed much later than that. The bar's large front window was decorated with a net of blinking Christmas lights that alternated to form circles and frills. The place was fairly quiet at that time of day, and the patrons weren't as young as I'd thought. I saw a pair of forty-somethings at the bar. The woman was chubby and sat with her legs crossed; she laughed spasmodically as the man whispered in her ear. At the back, I made out a couple of shadows by the pool table. The waitress, a girl with long, black hair who was cleaning bottles with a feather duster, looked at me for a few seconds. I realized that I was standing stupidly in the doorway. Embarrassed, I quickly left, bought something to eat and made it to my room, evading the mulatta as best I could.

On the 26th, Mariola and the baby were transferred to the Siete Puertas prison. An officer informed me when I signed in at the station that morning. He wasn't the handsome cop. He was new, and looked like a retiree who was possibly filling in for somebody off for the holidays. He smiled at me and explained that my sister could have visitors, although he didn't know how many or what I had to do. He recommended that I go there directly to find out. Siete Puertas was a quiet jail, he said, and it was a good thing because she didn't have anywhere else to go after all, so I shouldn't worry. It'll all turn out okay, he added.

"And how long do I have to stay here like this?" I asked.

"Not long, I don't think. We'll let you know tomorrow. They're having a meeting about your case later."

That lifted my spirits. When I left the station, Cárdenas seemed cleaner and sunnier than ever. Tired of window shopping and trying on clothes I couldn't buy, I thought it would be a good idea to visit one of the museums. My parents would probably ask if I'd gone to any, and would think it was strange if I hadn't. Maybe I could bring them a postcard or keychain as proof. I chose the museum that housed Spanish paintings because I knew where it was, thanks to my walks, but I chose poorly: it cost eight euros to get in, and later I found out that the majority of the museums were free. Besides, I didn't think what I saw was very interesting. I stopped in front of each painting, counted to ten, and moved on to the next. There were lots of rooms and the tour was starting to bore me. I took too long in the first part, where there'd only been tiny gold-framed paintings of Virgin Marys with ashy skin, angels in brocade tunics, and old man-faced Baby Jesuses. I started to go more quickly after that. The last rooms were full of furiously-painted canvases where you could see brushstrokes, dollops, rust-colored metal sheets, rope, and stuff like that. The piece that struck me most was of a man cut in half, one side totally healthy—and wearing half a suit—and the other bloody, all muscles and frayed tendons. There were lines of ants in his wounds and lots of blue flies, too. The color of the blood reminded me of the pomegranate, and I realized I hadn't thought about it all day. I felt good.

When I finished at the museum, I sat outside on a bench and ate another sandwich as I watched a gang of pigeons fight over the most minimally edible scrap. It had gotten late all of a sudden and it was pretty cold again, so I decided to put off the trip to Siete Puertas until the next day.

I started to feel unwell. My forehead was burning and I had chills all over. Despite how I felt, I went the round-about way so I could walk past the Oasis. Through the big window I saw a woman sitting alone at the bar. She had very short hair and sparkly, tight pants, and there were three guys in dress clothes who seemed to be doing important business in the back. The Christmas lights, with their blinking, rhythmic series of shapes—frills, circles—made me feel dizzy and nauseous.

I went straight to bed, after crossing inevitable paths with the manager. She stared at me.

"You gotta bad look. You better not get sick on me and screw us, you hear?"


I did get sick. I had to struggle to get out of bed and go sign in at the station, where the same officer, the old, retired cop, asked me if I was feeling okay. I nodded wordlessly. I had a terrible sore throat. My nose was leaking and my bones felt like they were about to break.

"I asked about your case yesterday," he said, becoming very serious.

I gave him a questioning look.

"It's still not certain, but you'll most likely only have to come four or five more days."

He lowered his voice and glanced around.

"The commissioner who deals with these things is on vacation. He's back on the second."

"Does that mean I have to spend New Year's Eve here? I'm almost out of money for the hostel."

"I don't know what it means, my dear. And don't think I'm not sorry about it. All I can do is pass on what I know."

I signed in and I went back to my room. I slept the whole day, a deep sleep plagued with scenes that included a multitude of people I couldn't remember later. In the afternoon, I gathered the strength to go out and buy aspirin. Sharp pain pierced my head; my eyes were liquid with fever. I stopped in front of the Oasis again on the way back. I studied the door with a sense of vertigo. I couldn't see clearly what was happening inside, but it looked lively. Latin music was playing, or something that sounded like Latin music. I put one foot inside the door, stumbled, and backed away. The image of the pomegranate hit me in the face: a red lamp spinning farther back, suspended over the dance floor. A guy with a mustache asked me if something was wrong. I don't remember what I said. I think I just turned around. I went up to my room, took two aspirin, and slept like a log.

I woke up hungry, with nothing to eat in the room. I was still weak, though not as bad as the day before. Waiting for me at the station this time was the handsome cop, with his arhythmic, ridiculous voice. He gave me a hard look. He was probably mad about something that had nothing to do with me.

"To be honest, I'm surprised you haven't asked how José de la Cruz's family is doing."

I stammered.

"How are they? Did he have kids?"

The officer pegged me with a look of disdain.

"You don't even stop and think about what you're saying. What do you mean, does he have kids? He was going to adopt your nephew because he couldn't have them, remember?"

I ducked my head and signed. Tears surged behind my eyes. I wasn't guilty of anything, I told him, and my sister wasn't either. It had been self-defense.

"Yeah, we know your version of events, but that doesn't convince anybody. Now listen here," he added. "You can go home whenever you want, but you've got to be ready to come to Cárdenas when you're called. If you don't, you'll be arrested. And you can't leave the country. Understood?"

"I didn't plan on leaving the country."

"I didn't ask you what you planned to do or not. I'm just telling you what you have to do, got it?"

"Got it."

"Good, you can go."

As I turned to leave, I heard him call me.

"Wait a minute. Here."

Grudgingly, he filled out a form and handed it to me.

"You can visit your sister at Siete Puertas today, this here is an authorization. The pass is only valid for today, for you to use before you go. Hand it in at the first window, with your ID, all right?"

"All right."

I folded the paper in half and stuck it in my coat pocket. Then I looked him full in the face. His eyes were brown, big and clear like those of an intelligent dog. But he was still in a bad mood. He impatiently drummed his fingers on the table, waiting for me to leave. So I did, a little disappointed. A little, but not very: at least I was lucky enough to be able to call my parents and tell them I'd be coming home the next day. They'd still be angry at me and I'd pay for it when I got home, but at least I'd be there. The shop would be open on the 29th, the 30th, and the 31st until noon. There was still time to atone for my guilt through work.

But there was definitely no time to go to Siete Puertas. It had to be outside the city and I was still getting over being sick. I still had to pack my bag, call my parents, buy tickets at the train station, take a little time to think and all that. And I felt uneasy about leaving the part of Cárdenas I knew so well, about going to see Mariola in that jail and not knowing what to do or what to say to her. I didn't even have the money to buy a present for my nameless nephew. No, I wouldn't go. It wasn't worth it.

Between one thing and another, the afternoon passed. I told the manager of the hostel that it was my last night and we'd square up in the morning. As usual, her lip curled with mistrust.

My mother answered the phone. When I announced my return, she didn't show delight. More like irritation, an eagerness to carp on about how things couldn't be patched up so easily after all that. She was wry. For all she cared, I could stay in Cárdenas as long as I liked, but I'd better not even think about returning home when the money ran out. She told me I had to follow my conscience, and if my conscience allowed me to sleep at night, it was because I was no good.

She also said she didn't need me at all, but quickly added that they were buried by orders and my selfishness had no limits. I tried to placate her. My arguments didn't matter. I felt no relief when we hung up.

Afterward, I went to buy a train ticket. I had to wait in a long line. I wanted it to be over, but with the ticket in hand, I felt a terrible emptiness. All of a sudden I had no idea what I was doing there, or what I needed to do next. I killed some time looking at a few sculptures on display in the central halls of the station. I went to the bathroom and was annoyed that I had to pay to use it. Then I browsed the shopping area, looking at junk: toys, Christmas ornaments on sale, knock-off perfume, chocolates, T-shirts, and boots, more slouchy leather boots with a bow like mine. I stole a lipstick from the cosmetics shop. My heart was racing, but not because of the lipstick. I had to ask an old couple if I could sit next to them because there were no free benches. First, they scooted over, but then immediately got up and left grumbling. I held my head in my hands. I didn't care anymore who looked at me or looked away. Something squeezed my temples, something greater than my numbness and shame. A woman with blueish hair stopped in front of me, she didn't speak. She moved on, shaking her head in disgust. I tried to control my breath. I stretched my legs, exhaled a few times, and—gradually—the attack passed.

I thought my last night in Cárdenas ought to be different. I was hungry and felt like having something besides the same old sandwiches. Could I do it? Go into a bar and eat alone, as

I'd seen other girls do, with all their self-confidence and ease? I wandered around the area near the Avenida de la Constitución but didn't have the guts to go into any of the restaurants clustered along the sidewalk. Everyone appeared to be in good company: laughter, glint of glasses clinked together for a toast, foam-topped beers, all the things that belonged to other people and not to me. I lost my nerve and went to VIPS again. I had a burger with egg, melted cheese, lettuce, and tartar sauce, and a ton of fries that I devoured as I stared at my plate. My table was out-of-the-way. I felt okay at first, but then I started feeling anxious and tired and wanted to get out of there as soon as possible.

I left and walked in the direction of the Oasis, shuffling my feet. I wasn't ready to go back to my room; I didn't think I could stand another night like that. It was only nine and I had a full stomach and all my tasks complete. A cold vapor rose from the ground, a kind of nocturnal mist that made me shiver. I stuck my hands in my pockets and that's when I remembered the visitor's pass for the prison. I couldn't let my parents find it. I tore it up and threw it in the trash.

It was Friday and the Oasis was unusually busy. I paused in the doorway, like I'd always done. But this time, I sensed a group of people behind me, getting closer and pushing. I got a whiff of various perfumes.

"Excuse me."

They were spics, spics like there were everywhere in Cárdenas. They passed by me and went inside: a group of squat men and women, dark, with flat foreheads and wide teeth. I followed them without realizing what I was doing and then felt weird going back out. I went to the bar and saw a couple order rum and Cokes. I asked for the same. The girl who served me smiled as she looked right through me, like I was transparent. She had a head of exotic, curly hair and was dressed completely in black and showing a lot of cleavage. She also wore big, long earrings. The sight of her made me feel awful.

"That's seven euros."

I only had a ten on me. I hadn't imagined a drink would cost so much, especially at a place filled with spics. But so it was. I paid and sat down on a stool, watching the door and pretending I was waiting for someone. I drank my rum and Coke with small sips; I wanted to make it last as long as possible. I observed the group that had just come in. Together they formed a continual wave of giggles and batting eyelashes: some were clearly flirting with each other. Maybe they were all flirting. More people were sitting at the bar in the back, others playing darts. There was a table where a small group of women talked in low voices, very seriously. Shadows and red lights, *the pomegranate, gnawed and split-open and eternal,* a red, hazy atmosphere encompassing the world. I was the only person who was alone. I got out my phone and typed aimlessly. I didn't even have a cigarette to smoke. When I looked up, there was a heavy guy beside me, with creamy skin and small eyes and freckles.

"Are you waiting for somebody?"

"Yeah . . . um . . . yeah."

He looked me over. He was younger than me, seventeen or eighteen at most. A strange look of scorn puckered his lips. He let out a soft, mocking laugh.

"Then I'll go."

"No, don't go," I said. I lowered my voice. "Actually, I was getting bored."

He sat down next to me. He had trouble climbing onto the stool he was so fat. When he was finally situated, a layer of pudge spilled over his groin. His arms were bare. They reminded me of raw bread dough.

"Aren't you cold?"

"Not in here. I left my jacket over there."

He nodded toward a coat rack.

Then he told me that his name was David and he lived in Bocancha. He worked at a computer store and he had just had a fight with his boss because he hadn't given him one *fucking* day off for the holidays. His boss was named Ramírez; then there was another partner named Castro and three other employees as well, not counting Sole, who was just at the store to look good. Ramírez and Sole were involved, he told me; that explained everything. In terms of suppliers, they hadn't stopped shipping merchandise to the shop because Castro insisted over and over that this was the best sales time of the year. For him, maybe, David added, he didn't have to fill out delivery notes all afternoon. I listened to him without asking any questions, I saw how he talked and talked—spit accumulating in the corners of his mouth—and I started to get lost in his stories of abuse, injustice, persecutions, and ambushes. David spoke with his head down, in a very quiet voice, tripping over his words. He was hard to understand.

"Can you buy me a drink?" he asked suddenly.

I stammered. "I barely have any money. See, I came with ten euros and this cost seven."

"A beer here is two-fifty."

He ordered one from the waitress. When she'd served him, he took a sip and continued: "I came straight from the warehouse, I don't even have a cord on me. But I can buy you a drink another day, if you want."

I explained that I was passing through Cárdenas, that I was leaving the next day. He nodded very solemnly and then kept talking as if he hadn't heard.

"I know a great place, better than this, over in Boliches. I'm friends with Fede, one of the waiters, a stand-up dude. We could go tomorrow."

"I'm leaving Cárdenas tomorrow afternoon."

"Fine, Sunday then. They're open on Sundays, too."

He rolled his eyes and changed his tone.

"Hey, let me know if I'm bothering you, okay?"

"You're not bothering me."

"You sure? Tons of girls say that, but then they slap you if you try and put your arm around them."

"You aren't bothering me, honest."

"But you have a boyfriend, eh?"

He drank more beer.

"Do you? Have a boyfriend?"

"Yeah, but he isn't here."

"You're not waiting for him?"

"No."

He moved his stool closer to mine and brought his lips to my ear. He stank of alcohol. My beer wasn't the first one he'd drunk that night.

"Then I can tell you that you're really hot."

I pulled away nervously and looked around us. The group of spics had moved to the back of the club and two of them, a short little man and a very brown woman with a big ass, danced slowly on the gold stage, bathed in the light from the gnawed and split and eternal pomegranate. The man ran his hands slowly over the woman's ass and she swung her hips, her head turned to one side.

The rest, I believe, is what people tend to do in such cases, although I don't have much experience, and even less when it comes to how they do things in Cárdenas. We stayed a little longer, sipped our drinks until they were finished, exited into the cold night. He put his arm around my shoulder and I didn't slap him. I knew then that I was going to lose my virginity to that boy and I thought how, if it had to happen like this, it was better to get it over with. We kissed clumsily. His tongue was rough and sharp. I was assailed by a sense of urgency to get it over with. I told him I was staying nearby and suggested he come with me.

Despite all that, the worst part of sleeping with him wasn't anything we did. Actually, I don't remember what we did, or if we talked afterward or not, or what time he snuck out of the room and finally let me sleep. The worst part was the next morning when, as she leaned against the doorjamb, the manager reminded me that the price "with muchacho" was double. And her scowl when I gave her the money: her curled lip and bloodshot eyes, half-hidden by gross, thick eyelids that, say what you will, us white people just don't have.

# PAPÁ IS MADE OF RUBBER

IN FELT SLIPPERS, her hair tousled and damp, the neighbor throws open the door to apartment 3A and steps onto the dim landing. Minute violet blemishes dot her checks. Her nostrils flare.

"I'd rather be called a busybody than do nothing!" she says.

Through the half-open door slips a man's voice revealing more exhaustion than deference.

"Do whatever you want. You always do want you want anyway."

The woman marches to end of the hallway and stops in front of 3B. She lifts her hand to press the doorbell buzzer, but then slowly lowers it and glances behind her. The murmur of the television is a sign that her husband considers their argument over. She sighs, turns back to the door, and rings. First, a quick press; then, after several seconds with no acknowledgment, she holds down the button. Though she strains her ears, she can't hear anyone inside, no response, no movement: nothing.

As she's just about to leave, the door opens brusquely, as if somebody had been standing behind it all along. A boy of about eleven fixes his huge dark eyes on the neighbor woman who, slightly flustered, stammers a question.

"Hello, Dani . . . Can I speak to your parents?"

"My mom isn't here right now," he says, as if preoccupied. His voice, while still child-like, is inflected with a solemness unusual for his size. "I'll see if papá wants to come out," he adds. "If you'll just wait a minute . . ."

Daniel disappears into the shadows of the apartment. The neighbor observes, through the door separating the foyer from the entrance, bulky, unidentifiable shapes scattered down the long hallway. When her eyes adjust to the darkness, she discovers that the shapes are toys, stacks of paper, small mounds of clothing strewn in corners. Only then does she spy the other child at the end of the hall. Though she can't see him clearly, she assumes it must be the middle child, Andrés. He is engrossed, humming a little song to himself and dragging what looks like a little gadget on wheels across the floor. Despite the chaos and mess, the apartment smells good, like toast and warm pâté, the aroma of an after-school snack that briefly makes her doubt herself. Then Daniel reappears, with the serious expression of a child who knows he's the firstborn.

"Papá says he'll speak with you later. He can't interrupt what he's doing right now. That's what he said." The boy scratches his ear and looks at the floor. "He can't."

"Fine, okay." She hesitates. "Dani, are you all okay?"

As Dani nods, well-mannered and polite, Andrés approaches silently, shuffling his feet in their wrinkled socks, a finger up his nose. The neighbor looks at him and sees that what he's been scraping all over the floor isn't a train or a car or any other toy, but a small, bug-eyed hamster, which he holds tightly in his dirty fist. Andrés shows her and she can see that the animal has a bloody streak running the length of its skinned belly. Suppressing a gag, the neighbor whips around and returns to her safe and comfortable home, slamming the door behind her.

Daniel leans against the doorjamb, the baby on his hip, and watches Andrés get ready for school. Andrés is slow. He gets distracted, leaves the zippers on his backpack undone, can't tie his shoelaces right. Daniel watches him in silence, cradling the baby, until Andrés looks up and their eyes meet.

"You're going to be late again."

"Why aren't you coming?"

Churlish, Andrés flops down on the unmade bed and turns to face the wall. With a small bitten fingernail, he lifts the edge of a ragged piece of the tape holding up a Pokémon poster.

"You know why. Someone has to stay and take care of Luca."

The baby fusses and Daniel shifts positions, whispers something into his neck. Andrés picks at the tape.

"We could take turns. One day you, then me. I can take care of him, too. I'm seven, you know."

"Come on," Daniel is firm. "You're going to be late."

Andrés sits up on the bed and returns to tying his laces.

Daniel takes the baby to the kitchen, where he sits him in a highchair and absently strokes his head. He rummages through the pots and pans piled in the sink, looking for the bottle, then rinses it out and puts a pot of water to heat on the stove. The sun has just risen and the light entering through the laundry room is hazy, pinkish, and vaguely depressing. A thread of orderly ants march along the edge of the countertop. Daniel kills them one by one with his finger as he listens for the sound of the front door opening and closing, the sound of the wheeled backpack hitting each stair, and the small steps as they get farther away.

Suddenly, he runs to the living room. He's grabbed a small, irregularly-shaped tinfoil packet from the little kitchen table. He opens the window and shouts down to Andrés. The little brother looks up apathetically from below.

"You forgot your snack!"

He tosses the sandwich down to the sidewalk, where Andrés doesn't manage to catch it. The packet tumbles down the pavement. Daniel sees it bounce and spin until Andrés stops it with his foot. Then he hears the baby crying alone in the kitchen.


From the doorway, Andrés observes his father lying in bed. Daniel insists that he's really sick. Andrés is only allowed to see him from here, they don't want to wear Papa out, Daniel says. His father doesn't speak, doesn't move, doesn't even wave hello. He seems inhumanly stiff; his skin dull, drawn. He wears a baseball cap sporting an advertising slogan. Daniel, who is allowed to sit with him, holds Papa's fingernail-less hand and speaks in a low voice. The room is always dark. Andrés can barely make out the shape of the bed, the closet, the nightstand, the exercise bike that, in other times, his mother rode to keep in shape.

"When's he going to get better?" Andrés asks.

"Soon," says Daniel. "He's still sick but he's getting better. This morning he got up for a little while. He played with Luca in the living room."

"He always gets up when I'm at school. I never see him."

"You'll see him soon."

Daniel stands and covers their father's body with the sheet. Papa is still. Andrés's eyes well up and he gives little kicks at the floor.

"Why are you locking the door?"

"I'm not. This is just a little wire to close the latch from the outside. Papa asked me to."

"How come?"

"He doesn't want anyone going in without permission."

"Nobody? Why do you get to go in and I can't?"

"I don't know. No one can go in. That's just how he wants it."

Andrés follows Daniel to the living room. They sit beside the crib where the baby is sleeping. The floor is littered with dirty diapers, Playmobile figurines, scraps of food. In the corner, one plant is drying up and another is completely withered. Andrés opens the hamster's cage and shakes a little water from the baby bottle into the food dish. Then, with the rodent in his hand, he murmurs.

"The neighbor lady came again when you were out shopping yesterday. I told her papá was in the shower and mamá was out with you on a walk."

Daniel looks up.

"Good, good. You did good."

"But," he adds, "better not to answer the door next time."

Daniel goes to the supermarket in the evening, when Andrés can stay with Luca and there's less of a chance that someone will ask why he isn't in school. He knows he shouldn't be out too long; even so, he loiters among the shelves as if he were taking a leisurely stroll. He knows where all the security cameras are located and how the light blinks if someone is watching. He also knows that there's nobody behind most of the cameras, but he still doesn't risk it. If he sees something he wants in a danger zone, he puts it in the shopping basket and only later, once he's beyond the reach of the camera's penetrating eye, he slips it into one of the inside pockets of his big coat. First, he makes sure that the item in question doesn't have a sensor, and if it does, he scrapes it off with his nail. He keeps the cheaper items in his basket and puts the more expensive ones in his coat, but this isn't always an easy rule to follow. In any case, he knows he must save money. There isn't much left.

Today, he has hidden a wedge of cheese, two small cans of tuna, a package of gummy candies, and a chocolate bar. The basket has yogurt smoothies, muffins, and bread. He holds a canister of baby formula, lost in thought. It's too expensive to put in the basket, but too big to try to hide in his coat. He picks it up and sets it down several times. He walks away and stops to think at the back of the store, where they stack the rolls of toilet paper and boxes of diapers. There's no security back there. Daniel returns for the formula, and while pretending to tie his laces, removes the silver packet of powdered milk from the can and stuffs it in a pocket. Just then, he sees the reflection of a blue uniform behind him. He turns slowly. It's only a stock boy, a kid who hasn't even registered his presence. He feels better when a cashier's voice pages someone over the loudspeaker. The blaring, he thinks, will protect him from getting caught.

Daniel has chosen the checkout with the longest line, where a diminutive cashier with long, skinny arms quickly scans the items and puts them in bags with mechanical precision. People tend to look at him kindly—a kid, doing the shopping!—but this is not at all to his benefit. He would prefer to pass completely unnoticed. His heart hammers as if it's about to explode out of him and he crosses his hands over his chest to hold it in. When it's his turn, the cashier smiles at him and starts to move his items along the conveyor belt. Daniel pays quickly and exits the store, unable to suppress an anxious giggle. For a lot less money than usual, he's bringing home food for at least three or four days.

In the main vestibule, he finds the gas deliveryman ringing their apartment. The man is sweating and in a hurry. He's not the least surprised when Daniel goes up and then returns with the money on his own.

"You don't have to bring the gas up," he tells the deliveryman. "My father will come down for it in a minute."

This is fine by the deliveryman and he leaves without a word of thanks. Daniel exhales. He feels tired, but proud of himself, too: just like he managed to haul the mannequin from the dumpster, now he'll have to haul the gas cylinder upstairs. He takes the grocery bags up first, and then, tenaciously pulls the heavy cylinder over to the elevator. He's on edge, panting, by the time he gets it into the kitchen. He leans over the counter to rest and smiles at Andrés coming down the hallway to greet him, a headless Action Man in his hand.

It's siesta time. Specks of light filter through the closed blinds into the darkened room, lit only by colors emitted from the television. The boys are plopped down on the rug watching afternoon cartoons. Even the baby pays attention, patting the floor happily and babbling with bubbly little noises, turning side to side when the white walls reflect the blue and green lights of the screen. Spread on the floor in front of Andrés are several workbooks, a textbook with creased edges, chewed pencils, a compass, and a ruler. Despite the mess, there's something stable about the scene. The brothers alternate between laughter and quiet, steered by the adventures of the little clay penguins moving about on screen. Everything seems solid.

Then the doorbell buzzes. A strident, threatening sound. Daniel takes the remote and lowers the volume gradually until they are left in dense silence. Several seconds go by and the buzzer sounds again, with an insistence that roots all three children to the floor. The baby fusses and Andrés moves to cover his mouth. Daniel, meanwhile, crawls down the hallway on his hands and knees. He is startled midway by a third long, loud buzz. He halts momentarily, then continues to the door, where he sits, ear pressed against the wood. He knows he can't look through the peephole because then *they* will know that the brothers are inside. Anyway, they *already* know they're inside, he thinks. He can hear them say it, hear them speculate about when they'll be able to force the door. Somebody claims they heard the TV, somebody else declares that it's been way too long since any adult has been seen around there; a third person whispers that maybe the children have been abandoned. Daniel recognizes the neighbor lady's warbling voice claiming that it was the mother who disappeared first, then the father. Maybe she was having an affair, she says, and he lost his mind. Daniel hears them leave. He rests his forehead on the door and stays there a while, hugging his shaky knees.

When he returns to the living room, he sees the baby has a handkerchief tied over his mouth. He runs to him, rips it off, and punches Andrés in the chest.

"Are you crazy?" he whispers. "He could suffocate!"

The two brothers scuffle in silence while the overtired baby fusses.


Daniel stands on tiptoe and feels around the top shelf of the kitchen cabinet. He runs his hand across the length of it, but only manages to get his fingers covered in dust, sugar, and spilled breadcrumbs. Rattled, he gets a stool to have a better look. The piece of wire isn't where it should be. He swears softly and searches the whole kitchen. At last he finds it sitting on top of a glass jar containing a few traces of flour. He grabs the piece of wire and thinks.

"Andrés! Andrés, did you take the . . . ?"

Andrés calls back from the living room.

"What?"

"Nothing." Daniel shakes his head and gets down from the stool. "Nothing."

Silence follows, then Andrés's voice again, thinned by the distance.

"When's mamá coming back?"

"I don't know," Daniel says. And seconds later: "Soon."

"Will she be back before they come for us?"

"No one's coming for us. Why did you say that?"

"They asked about you at school today."

"Who asked about me?"

"A couple of big kids. They asked why you're never in class anymore."

"What did you tell them?"

"I told them that you had a fever."

"Good. That's good." Daniel sits on the stool and covers his face with his hands.

He stands, makes his way to the bedroom, and uses the wire to jimmy the lock. In the dark, shrouded in the solitude and emptiness, the body in repose. Daniel calls Andrés and tells him to bring the baby so that he can see, too. As they come in, he sits on the bed and pretends that the inert figure can still work as their father. Andrés appears in the doorway with the baby. He's quiet and impassive this time; he doesn't attempt to approach the bed. Daniel looks up and hears Andrés speaking very slowly, very calmly, as if what he was saying had no importance at all.

"Papá is made of rubber."

Daniel stands and goes to him. He doesn't speak; he looks into his eyes, just inches from his face.

"Papá is made of rubber," Andrés says again. "Hard rubber. Plastic, whatever. It's not really papá. I already saw."


This time, they don't even have time to turn down the volume. They ate lunch on the rug and are happily letting their lunch settle. Daniel tried his hand at sausages and mash and Andrés is happy, he's on his back with his hands on his belly, the empty plate beside his legs. He isn't giving much thought to the ruse. Maybe it's better like this, he thinks, maybe they should keep the charade going. If clay penguins can exist, why can't papás be made of rubber? The baby gums a biscuit and smiles at the images on the screen. Daniel is half asleep and doesn't hear the voices outside of the door. There's no warning this time, no buzzing of the bell. They jump at the sound of the sharp blow to the lock, the splintering of wood, the authoritative, virile voices of two or three men speaking purposefully. Andrés gets to his feet in alarm, seeking his brother's eyes. But Daniel has hardly moved. He merely stretches out one arm, all but relieved now, and runs his fingers softly down the baby's neck. The baby giggles at his touch. It's over, he whispers. The voices advance down the hallway and the penguins talk about a party they're throwing in an igloo. The footsteps hasten in the hall and the penguins laugh. The commotion is terrible but Daniel, Andrés, and the baby are silent. The penguins sled over the snow.

# WHAT IS GOING ON WITH US?

THEY WERE YOUNG WOMEN, not a couple of twenty-year-olds, sure, but still, he had almost three decades on them. He invited the two of them out for fish—fish, he said, as if it weren't possible to order anything else—at a small restaurant near the office, one he obviously has been going to his whole life with his wife or various lovers, based on the way they greeted him when they arrived. Familiarity, professionalism, subordination: the waiter knew what guys like him expected when they walked through the door. The three were brought to the table in the back, they allowed their coats to be taken, they got comfortable. The chef came out to say hello, called the man by his name, and observed his two companions with discreet appreciation. Their ingredients were market-fresh, he said, and today this or that. The man cut him off. Don't waste our time with nonsense, he said. Just bring us the best fish you've got. These girls deserve nothing less. The best, he repeated. And the best wine, too. The chef nodded and asked if they wished to begin with an appetizer. Anchovies, the man interrupted. They wanted anchovies. Very well, said the chef.

Anchovies. With a little tomato, sliced avocado, on rustic baguette, or . . . ? The man raised his voice. Just the anchovies, for God's sake, good anchovies don't need anything else. He waved his hand smugly. The chef retreated, smiling, head slightly bowed. The girls exchanged glances and shrugged. They were amused. That man, one of the company's founders, an old fox who knew every trick in the book, was still their boss and they observed him from a remove. They admired him, nonetheless, in their own way. The girls—ironic, jolly, and not exactly innocent—didn't tend to put anybody on a pedestal. They pretended to make fun of everything, and even though that included him, they also valued his cynicism, his dark humor, his shamelessness. Now the three of them laughed at the table, while he discussed—criticized—everybody— especially the women—at the office, feeling better, smarter, sharper, above the mediocrity of the job. The girls spoke little and drank a lot.


She parks more or less close to home, maybe too close— realizing the neighbors can see her clumsy maneuvering. The bitter aftertaste is still between her teeth—she didn't even rinse her mouth—and she wobbles toward her door, which she doesn't manage to open on the first, or even the second, try—how ridiculous, she thinks, this is always how people imitate drunks. It's only on the third or fourth attempt that she gets it open, and when she steps inside, she is confronted by a green stain, a color she eventually associates with her husband's sweater, her husband, who is sitting on the couch with his laptop, beside their daughter, who is just starting her dinner—whatever I could find, he explains, nothing was prepared—and, unsettled by the luminosity of that green, she meets his worried eyes, his cracked smile, because he knows that she's coming home after being with someone else—he doesn't want to ask, is terrified to ask—and she, comforted by the lack of questions, goes upstairs to shower—I'm exhausted, she says—and thinks blearily about how wrong her husband is, just how off, if only the reason for his fear was real and she was actually back after meeting a lover, but she doesn't even try to dissimulate now, she just wants to wash herself, clean herself, she needs to wipe the disgust from her body. She yanks down her skirt and it falls to the floor, the long skirt she's always loved and now abhors. She stomps on it before stepping into the bath and turning on the faucet.

The girls spoke little and drank a lot. They laughed a lot, too, laughed loudly, complicit with the spectacle of the man regaling them with his catalogue of anecdotes. He knew this person and he knew that person, and he knew who was involved with whom, where they did it and for what dark reasons. He divided the women in the office into two groups: the ones he'd screw—that's how he said it, *screw*—and those he wouldn't—I'd rather do it with a monkey, he said. They, the girls, obviously belonged in the first camp. They all laughed again, roaring. My dears, he said, you are in the prime of your life, your thirties are absolutely the best decade. You're gorgeous, you're smart, you've got a past behind you and a future ahead. Life—and with this declaration, he lowered his voice—is not a straight path, you'll discover that for yourselves. Life is a labyrinth and it's tempting to lose yourself on its fringes, peripheral paths that might be mistakes or might be a good call; even if we always return to the middle, with all we've lived at the limits and without losing our way out, the way of success if possible, let's not kid ourselves, we have to try everything but only retain the essential, this is it, my dears, this is what it means to live, nothing more, nothing less, you'll discover it for yourselves in time, and the three of them raised their glasses and toasted again, filled them again, and the girls could guess what he meant by peripheral paths but they waved it off.

A group of five or six men in neckties had arrived and were sat at the next table. They appeared to be closing some kind of deal. The girls noticed the men looking at them. Mostly, one of the men looked at one of the girls, and occasionally she looked back, and everything was light, flippant, carefree, just like the old fox's conversation as he knocked back one drink after another—both his fondness and tolerance for alcohol were well-known—and now he was asking them about the most daring thing they'd ever done, although he was less interested in their responses than the chance to reveal his own. His eyes rolled back, he dampened his lips in anticipated pleasure of his story. Once, he said, at a wedding, the bride came to the top floor of the hotel during the reception and sucked his cock as they looked down on the groom from above. Like a movie, all of it, like a porno, he added, and the three laughed again, but the girls were starting to tire of that talk, of the bloated face, the veiny eyes and blue-blotched hands, and they hadn't even gotten to dessert.


But cleaning the upholstery in a high-end Audi like his, no, it's not that easy, not in an hour or two, for one thing, the odor treatment has to sit for a couple days, at least two if not three, then it has to be washed with foam disinfectant and dried with a stream of air to waterproof the leather and fabric and we just can't guarantee good results if we don't do it right, sure, no problem, the man can bring the car in, he'll wait in the shop for him, he can drop it off tonight and the guys will start on it first thing the next morning, if the man wants, he can send one of the guys out to get it if the man tells him exactly where it is, but he's got to understand that they can't do anything else at this time of night, the man's lucky he even reached anyone at the shop, they're squaring the register, otherwise the shop would've been closed, but the old fox says no, no he says, that's not how it's going to be, that's not what I'm saying, you don't get it, I'm telling you that I want that car spotless and I want it done now, and if that means that you put all your boys on the job then you do it, the old fox has never had a problem paying whatever it takes, has he ever had a problem paying? no, right? so then what the fuck is the problem, why all the hurdles, but still the mechanic continues to explain into the phone, the excuses spill over, their words overlap, and the old fox refuses to listen, he's leaning on the hood, the car doors open to air it out, the strong, acrid stink unrelenting, but this time his demands don't cut it, irate, he hangs up, insults dripping from his puckered lips, and the high-end Audi, not even a year old, the upholstery ruined, he curses, kicks the tire, swears again, a ways off someone is watching him, a shadow that won't stop him from kicking it a second time and ranting and raving until he tires.

They hadn't even gotten to dessert and they were already completely drunk. The man lit a cigar and one of the girls asked him whether they were allowed to smoke in there. Allowed? he repeated. Let's see, he said, and took a long puff. Behind the smoke, his eyes glinted in a new way. The men at the next table were watching more closely now, muttering among themselves. One of the girls got up to use the restroom and as she passed their table, tripped on her skirt, which was too long. Wobbling, she put her hand on one of the men's backs. Through his shirt, an unsettling warmth radiated. She apologized, straightened up as best she could, and, under a waiter's guidance, made her way in the direction of the restrooms. The men stared after her. The man she had touched smiled to himself, still sensing the hand between his shoulder blades.

Then they had one gin and tonic, then another. By the time they ordered a third round, the other men were gone. The waiter brought the drinks but hinted that the restaurant would be starting to close. The other girl blinked in surprise and looked at her watch. She should get going, too, she said. Her friend gave her a sidelong look. No, she said, don't go, and the old fox joined her pleas. Was she really going to leave now, when the three of them were having such a good time? Who cared if the restaurant was closing. They could go somewhere else, somewhere livelier. Were they really going to waste the marvelous evening ahead of them? The man's eyes gleamed more intensely now. He had loosened his tie and he pushed his chair back from the table, legs apart, at ease. That was when the string of lottery tickets paraded past and when they looked up, they saw the face with the dark glasses and purple birthmark on the cheek. "Tomorrow's drawing," the face announced. The voice was strident, feminine. "Three hundred thousand euros for tomorrow," he crooned. How'd they even let you in here? the old fox said, leaning back in his chair. Can't you see you're bothering us? The waiter hurried over. He's a friend of the house, he apologized, and whispered to the blind lottery seller to leave them alone, they're in the middle of something, he said. Meanwhile, the girl in the skirt was trying to convince her friend to stay, stay, she begged, leaning toward her. She couldn't stop laughing. "Lucky day tomorrow," repeated the man with the dark glasses, despite the waiter's intervention. A cackle from the old fox made the lottery seller retreat slowly, never turning his back. You think I need your luck? the old fox laughed. With these two beauties at my table? What do you know about luck, man? He finished his drink and turned toward the girl, the lottery seller already forgotten. She should stay, he said. Today more than ever. Hadn't she realized? They had luck in the palm of their hand.

Glassy eyes reflected in the mirror and she still stomps on the skirt, which is no longer a skirt but a jumble of dirty fabric that reminds her of roadkill. She leans against the edge of the sink, closes her eyes as tightly as she can, tells herself: think logically, think logically. Droplets slide down her cold, naked body, the skirt is getting soaked. She can hear the muffled sound of the TV, her daughter's high-pitched voice asking questions, her husband's monosyllabic answers, the clatter of fork on plate, eat up, you're almost done. She wants—she needs—to do something, it could be something as simple as sending a three-word text, or as immense as erasing a few hours of the past. Both possibilities seem equally feasible, but she can't face either. I'm not capable, she thinks, and it's then that her chin begins to quiver, she sinks to the floor and starts to cry with lethargy, almost with surprise.

They had luck in the palm of their hand, but the girl insisted that she had to go and the others insisted that she had to stay a little longer, just a little longer, and so another half hour went by, alcoholic and futile, during which time the chef came out to see how everything had been, making clear with strained elegance that there was nothing left for them to do there, now that the bill had been settled with cash pulled from the thick wallet, now that they'd already been served so many drinks, the lights off, evening falling on the other side of the window and yes, unfortunately, they had to lock up. Can you imagine, the old fox said to the chef, this lovely young lady wants to go home, right now, and the chef smiled wordlessly, while she slurred that her baby was only seven months old and must be missing her. Well, the old fox proposed, why didn't she go and see him, give him a bottle or whatever she had to do, and then come back out? Couldn't her husband handle the baby a little longer? Didn't they consider themselves feminists? Weren't they the type of girls who thought the man should be responsible for fifty percent of the childcare? They could take her home in a cab and wait for her downstairs, or at any of the bars in the area; it doesn't take long to warm up a bottle or change a few diapers. Yes, she agreed, that was a good idea, and the three stood up. The other girl smoothed her skirt rather gloomily, she knew her friend was lying. She wouldn't come back. When she put on her jacket, her sweater rose a few centimeters to expose a swath of skin where the waistband of her skirt clung lightly to her stomach. She noticed the man watching her. She smiled at him, but quickly lowered her eyes.

The next morning, she doesn't receive a single reproach, not a single question. She clandestinely pops pills for her hangover. Her temples pound and her eyes sting from crying, yet she can barely remember what happened: did she go straight to bed? did she say goodnight to her daughter? was she already asleep when her husband came in? did they talk, had he heard her sobs? She summons the strength to put on make-up, even so, the effort makes her hands shake. It's hopeless, she thinks, to try to conceal my swollen eyelids, the pallor of my dehydrated lips, my bloodshot eyes, it's hopeless if I'm going to have to see him anyway. And I'm going to have to see her, he thinks at pretty much the same time, sitting in his spacious kitchen, a kitchen three times the size of the girl's, with his wife across the table sipping from her cup, never glancing from her newspaper, and suddenly he lets it drop that he won't have the Audi for a few days, two or three at most, the motor was making a strange noise and he preferred to get it into the shop, but his wife doesn't respond, she doesn't show the slightest reaction, and only after a while, after he has repeated himself, maybe you didn't hear me, does she say do whatever you want, all I know is that you left the doors open the whole night, and now he's the one who doesn't respond, just like nobody responds to the goodbye the girl whispers as her husband steps into the hall to head to work—he always leaves a little before she does—the girl chews her lip and just when he's about to reach the door to the street, she steps onto the landing and asks him to come back up, please, she has to tell him something, and he pauses, thinks it over for several seconds that last for an eternity, and then he plods back up the stairs, takes her chin between his fingers, looks deep into her irritated eyes and asks her not to tell him, he prefers not to know, the same way that the old fox's wife raises her hand, as if to say no thank you, as she heads to another room in the chalet, she doesn't want to hear any explanations, she tells him, if the Audi has been open all night it's for a reason and I don't want to know, she repeats, all she asks is that he not lie, the motor making a noise, she laughs, we're too old to be dealing with such nonsense.

She quickly lowered her eyes as the old fox slowly, openly inspected her uncovered midriff until she tugged down her sweater, straightened her jacket, and walked off toward the exit with her friend, arm in arm, leaning against one another to compensate for their unsteadiness. The scarcity of light surprised them when they stepped out onto the sidewalk. It's almost nighttime! they exclaimed, and hurried—the old fox laboring after them—to a nearby taxi stand, where they got a cab that he paid for and which dropped them off close to the building where the baby had supposedly been waiting for several hours and whose mother bid them a hasty goodnight, practically running by then, leaving the two of them alone in a pub where she promised to return in just a little bit and where, obviously, she never did.

Seated on one of the high barstools, the remaining girl opened her legs to rest them on the bar footrest, spreading the fabric of her—still protective—skirt, while the old fox got closer, easing onto the barstool beside her—he's old, she thought, he has trouble getting up—and firmly ordering two dry martinis from a waiter who ignored him until he finished serving the other patrons. The girl said she preferred not to mix her alcohol and he started to laugh, but she'd already had two! Didn't she remember? They'd had wine, and cava, and then a couple of gin and tonics, and dry martinis, too. Had she really forgotten? You're gorgeous, he said, looking her in the eye, you have no idea how you shine in this horrible place. He tossed his head in a disparaging gesture that encompassed the whole bar. Look how low class, he said loudly, waiters aren't what they used to be, I would have taken you somewhere nice, somewhere in line with what you deserve, it's ridiculous that we even came here, your little friend's not coming back, she left us by ourselves for a reason. The girl laughed. For a reason? Yeah, and don't pretend you don't know what I'm talking about. I saw you two whispering. You were talking about me, weren't you? The old fox leaned in and kissed her neck. The girl shuddered, closed her eyes, laughed again. A row of small blue bulbs illuminated the interior of the glass bar, on which she could make out marks from other people's drinks. She pressed her fingers over the blue lights, one by one, playing an indolent game. He kissed her again and, still giggling, she asked him to stop, but he put his hand on her leg.

They're going to see each other and even though she gets there's no point in postponing it—after all, it will happen often over the coming days, weeks, months, years if she's lucky and they make her permanent—even though she knows it's best to display some degree of aloofness, a certain amount of indifference at least, she also feels like she needs a postponement, a delay, a retaining wall or fire break, just for a day, just not today, she doesn't want to see him today, not like other times when the elevator door opens and she goes in and he comes out, or she comes out and he goes in, not on the landing on the ground floor or the common areas or at the coffee machine or the café downstairs, and not in front of her desk, either, where he usually stops to say hello and observe her with a sardonic smile, certainly not today of all days, she pleads silently, not this morning. Nevertheless, he materializes right in front of her desk—since the old fox fears nothing, avoids nothing—looking at her out the corner of his eye today, as usual, but this time there's no smile, he stares, his expression sullen, knuckles on her desk, white knuckles, he's pressing his fists down hard on the tabletop and the knuckles are blanched—she notes the age-spots—and she continues typing, she doesn't look up, she types for a few seconds that feel like minutes, not because she wants to send a message of repulsion, but because her mind has gone blank and she can't do anything but keep typing and hope that he moves off. But he doesn't move off. He stays as long as necessary for her to give up, stretch her fingers, bring her breath under control as she sits still in expectation. He speaks. How are you, he asks. Fine, she replies shortly, not brusquely, though, because her disgust is so intense that it nullifies any possibility of hatred. I think we should talk later, he says. About what. Later I said, not now. About the car? The old fox clucks his tongue in annoyance. Forget the car, he says. The girl whispers weakly that they have nothing to discuss, and if what he wants is for her to pay for the car to be cleaned, that's fine, she'll pay every last cent. He turns and departs with a growl. Only then does the girl look up and watch him walk away, hunched, his bowed legs, the tennis shoes he wears on non-meeting days, and she can't contain the sob, nor the tears.


But he put a hand on her leg and without really knowing what she was doing—her actions contradicted her halting words—she offered him her neck again and then her lips and finally her tongue, and she felt strangely aroused, not physical arousal but something closer to mental excitement, and she felt wrapped in an inexplicable lightness, too, in the sweet impression that neither time nor space existed, as if she were entering a kind of peace where nothing she did had any consequence, a groundless path through a suggestive, appealing darkness, twinkling, too—starlit—but maybe that was just the blue lights of the bar. She kissed him without desire for his mouth, but with an insatiable desire to kiss, she saw everything through an opaque veil and yet she experienced a moment of sobriety when she saw, advancing toward her pupils, the extraordinarily fine web of violet veins on that man's nose, veins brought into unpleasant focus in a sudden but fleeting awareness, and she saw that man was kissing her, his body ever closer and she recalled that the man had invited them out for fish—both of them, but where was her friend?—and that he was one of founders of the company and that he divided women into two groups and that he scorned the idea of eating bread with good anchovies and he believed he had luck in the palm of his hand, when in reality his hands were open and he took her by the back of the neck with one of those palms and with the other rubbed her thigh through her skirt.

Then he scooted even closer and lifted her skirt up to her knees and stuck his hand in and got all the way up, and the girl was afraid he was going to do it right there in front of everyone, where anyone could see, but the thought was forgotten because at the same time she forgot the notions of "it," "there," and "in front of," just like she forgot how they got up and out of the bar, because suddenly they were on the sidewalk—he clutched her waist—and then quickly in another cab, where he lifted her skirt again and she closed her eyes so as not to meet the cabdriver's gaze in the rearview mirror. There were questions as well. Why not, what was the problem, and she said no, no, not entirely clear on what it was she was refusing. He mentioned a hotel, then a chalet outside the city he had for sale, and finally he said parking garage and in an instant there they were, in a parking garage, red lights indicating the taken spots, green for open, the contrast of white and red stripes in the corners assaulting her retina and the squeak of their boots on the floor. She stopped short. My car isn't here! she yelled. He told her not to yell. I'm not yelling! she yelled. The old fox laughed. Yes, he said. You are, you just don't realize it. Then he said not to worry. He would take her to her car later, but first they were going to sit in his for a little while until the dizziness wore off—the dizziness, he said, when she hadn't been aware of being dizzy. You didn't have to yell, he added smoothly. In fact, it was better if they were nice and quiet.

He took out the key fob and asked if she liked the Audi. She didn't understand the question. What Audi? she repeated, climbing inside. She fumbled nervously to recline the seat, complaining compulsively all the while, as he lifted the lever to help her. She lay back and was quiet for a few minutes, until she felt the man's hand creeping again and a sudden wave of nausea wracked the whole length of her body. He kissed her hair, told her to relax, and kept going. His fingers invaded deeper and deeper and she wanted to end it as quickly possible. She closed her legs. Don't be shy, he insisted. Let go. So she moaned. She moaned and moaned and moaned until it seemed sufficiently convincing. Okay, that's good, she whispered, repressing another gag. Let's go now, she pleaded.

He smiled. His shiny eyes smiled. The tiny veins on his nose smiled. His wet lips smiled. His wrinkled hands smiled. His smile was in no hurry. Were they really not going to go? she thought. She moved toward him and put her hand on his crotch. He shied away. She thought there was no other way to end that episode and insisted. His look, now, was supplicating. Under the fabric of his pants, nothing. Confused, she felt around, but in vain. Again, he removed her hand. I do the touching, he said. I touch, and I watch. With me, that's how it's done, he added, that's the deal, but she had no recollection of any deal. He kissed her softly and ordered her to rest a while. The girl pulled away to lie back down and that's when the third one came, the heave she couldn't repress, diaphragm contracted, throat tense, and then the stampede, the faucet, the smell everywhere, the sourness, limbs cold and shaking, and the name-calling as well, heard loud and clear, and after her apology, the names again.

She dashes out of the office because she doesn't want anyone to see her cry, her friend accompanies her, pretending to chat away as if this were a normal day, another day, whatever normal was, break time at a tedious office job like any other break at any other office, a trivial chat like any other, and she walks, damp eyes trained on the ground, rage amassing in the pit of her stomach, and once they're outside, she inhales deeply and stamps her boots on the sidewalk, notices that there are flecks of puke on her boots, too, flecks that speak for themselves, that betray her, and she laughs sadly, shaking her head, I don't know what I'm going to do. Nothing, says her friend, there's nothing you can do but forget it. They exchange a weighty look. Both have dark smudges under their eyes. They discussed the dark circles, as well on what happened with their respective arrivals at home, their respective children, respective husbands, dinners, beds, explanations, deceits, and silences. What's going on with us? they ask each other. Standing against the wall, engrossed in their cigarettes, they don't at first see the face with the dark glasses and purple birthmark, don't see it until the ream of lottery tickets passes before their eyes and then the lumbering blind man and the memory. They had never seen him before, and now, suddenly, twice in twenty-four hours. The fluty voice carries an unmistakable measure of disgust. "Tomorrow's drawing. Three hundred thousand euros for tomorrow." Each word is spit with derision. *Three hundred thousand euros.* His birthmark appears to have grown in just a day. It's strangely shaped, threatening. Behind the dark glasses, the girls notice, he is scrutinizing them. "Lucky day tomorrow." Simultaneously, the girls signal their rebuff and then simultaneously realize—they're smart girls, after all— that they've done exactly what the old fox did the day before, made the same gesture of disdain, arrogance, and contempt, but neither one mentions it.

# CATTLE TYRANTS

SHE WALKS HOME WATCHING the ground, her sneakers blotched by tears that haven't quite stopped falling. Her eyes sting. She walks home, the sun striking her naked shoulders, her sweaty neck. She isn't angry, or resentful; she's only afraid: afraid of getting home late. Alone. Without the bike.

"Where's the bicycle?" the aunts will ask.

"Where have you been?" they'll ask as well.

She'll have to think of an excuse. She forgot it on a street corner, she lent it to some kids who took it and disappeared.

It was stolen.

"Who stole it?" they'll ask, suspicious, clever.

That hateful cleverness, she murmurs to herself. The crazy, possessive, overprotective aunts. The aunts. The summer.

Nobody steals a bike in such a small village. In broad daylight. Without someone seeing, without someone doing something. They won't believe her. She quickens her pace, thinking of alternatives. She dries her tears, her eyes smart from the dust, the salt stings in the scratches on her forearm. Sting. She got covered in dirt when she fell. Her whole arm, her right knee, were badly scraped. Her pants stick to the wound, which throbs and bleeds a little. The stain spreads slowly. Dark brown on the worn blue of her jeans.

The long days, the cattle tyrants that watch her from the muck of the rice fields. The narrow, sandy path, flanked by reeds and tall, dry grasses. If she could just wash her hands. She knows the dirt smudges her cheeks every time she rubs her eyes. She's so dirty, they'll know she fell. She can't avoid them finding out in the end. It's hot, but she shudders. She fell. Okay, she'll admit that she fell.

But why had she ventured off so far? What was she doing on the paths out in the rice fields, outside of the village? She couldn't explain that. Where was the bike? Why didn't she have it with her? How was she going to explain the flat tire, the busted chain? How could she explain the reason she left it so far away, how heavy it was, how she could only manage to drag it for ten yards.

The wheel spinning slightly, the glint of the spokes under the August sun.

Their laughter in the background.

Her summers here, in the rice fields, while her friends enjoyed themselves at the beach, slathering on tanning oil in the sun, preparing themselves for the night's amusements.

Her summers here, her youth—her young blood—and the village she needs to escape, if only on an old bike with worn tires, if only to the paths in the rice fields where nobody goes. The forbidden, lonely paths where she can pedal fast, imagining, perhaps, if only for a fleeting moment, the taste of a freedom she doesn't know.

The paths where no one will see her, because no one's ever there, no one except the oxpeckers and field mice, the mosquitoes that dive bomb her arms and ankles, the occasional white-tailed kite soaring overhead in the bleached sky.

Nobody except the figures there, in the distance, by the embankment.

A small cluster beside an old car. Does she keep pedaling, or turn back?

"Don't trust people," the aunts always say. "Don't trust anyone."

And just why shouldn't she trust them? People by a car, still a way off, that's all they were. Two, maybe three of them? Two outside the car and one inside? Wasn't that a moped leaning against the stone wall? A moped, a car, three people?

She pedals closer and the inchoate group in the dust grows more defined. Her plan, when she reaches them, is to turn right, onto a new path, but no, she is not going to turn back. She will never turn back, why be so suspicious, why be forced to reverse course?

The boys watch her approach. Two of them stand beside the Renault Clio beat up by the country roads, one leaning on the battered hood. There's a third kid in the car, his arm resting on the partially unrolled window. Smooth smiles drip from their lips, from their mouths hungry for cruelty and action. They watch her and exchange a few words she can't hear because she's panting and pedaling even faster now that she has turned down the new path, and it's then, when her back is to them, that she feels the rock ricochet off the bike. She flinches and speeds up, and then comes the next rock, the rock that makes her lurch, take her hands off the handlebar, lose control, skid and crash into the dry grass and muck on the edge of the field.

And now she hurries home, her cut throbbing, her temples throbbing, her heart beating wildly, and the village finally begins to take shape in the shimmering waves of heat. The village, the aunts, the summer. How is she going to hide that she saw the boys' shoes when she was on the ground, how can she hide the rude laughter, the humiliating kick. The gleam of the pocketknife brought close to her face, then yanked back and plunged into the tire. The spinning spokes, the busted chain, her greasy, scraped arms, the relentless laughter. A hand grabs her breasts, first one, then the other, almost shyly, free from lust. She doesn't have time to be afraid. The bike, she thinks. The aunts. They stop groping her. They're afraid, too, because she doesn't move. She curls up, waits. They laugh harder, disconcerted, unsure what to do next. They might even be younger than she is. A couple of kids just starting to experiment, to test the waters. In this village, kids as young as ten drive on the lanes out in the rice fields with permission from their stupid, uneducated parents. The aunts said so.

"You mustn't go there, it isn't safe."

They had warned her. The damn aunts, she thinks, they're worse than the boys. The boys disappear and leave her lying at the edge of the muck, under the mute sun, under an apathetic God who never responds when needed most. Not even the cicadas' incessant hum can break the silence.

She gets up, brushes herself off, studies the bike. Impossible. She can't carry it so far. Nonetheless, she does try, without tears, at first, without complaint. But hastily, because of the time.

But she won't make it, she won't. She leaves the bike on the path.

The village is far but she's getting close. Her feet ache, the stain on her knee spreads, darker, reddish brown. Tell-tale. Her own doubts are worse than the dull, muted pain, worse than the stinging in her eyes.

What to tell the aunts now?

What to tell them?

# MUSTELIDS

WITHOUT EXPLANATION, SHE led him to the mounted animal exhibit several yards away. Over here, she had said, and silently, they went. When they'd passed through the arched entranceway and he saw the dead animals on display, he had turned to look at her in surprise.

"You're into taxidermy? Seriously?"

She shrugged, evasive.

"No. Yes. Not really. This is just the quietest spot."

The museum was overrun with children. Noisy troublemakers who roamed the halls, staircases, and exhibit rooms in packs, herded by overwhelmed teachers, parents, counselors, and nannies who were even more strident, more enthusiastic than the children at times, as they hauled knapsacks, cameras, snacks, activity books, and boxes of pencils that dropped on the floor, rolling and tripping other visitors. The attraction of the moment was the new exhibit of dinosaurs that moved and even roared, opening and closing their mouths with a lukewarm ferocity the children pretended to fear. The terrariums, 3-D movie theater, and game area—*the interactive zone*—were also in high demand: cranks, wheels, levers, and buttons to press, bite, rub, suck, or simply break.

They left the tumult behind and walked through the narrow hall lined on either side with specimens in glass cases. Desiccated, he murmured. He had a sense of passing into a holy temple where a small number of devotees pressed their noses to the glass with almost religious respect, reading about each species on little signs, under their breath, their lips barely moving.

They strolled through the exhibit, glancing sideways at the animals with their cold eyes and dull pelts. They didn't touch. It was their first time traveling together, and the trip had forced them into an unfamiliar intimacy. At the company, they were just another pair of employees—they didn't even work on the same floor. Now they had to walk side by side and try to hold a conversation. They had prepared for the meeting on the plane, discussed what their approach ought to be. There would be some people they didn't know in attendance, and likely some perplexed executives who would skeptically hear their proposals and later repeat them in different words, more inflated and pompous. They agreed on their focus, perhaps because neither one really cared about ceding or convincing the other. They were selling their work, that's it: they were both clear on that. He liked that she showed faint disdain toward her job. He thought that, in some way, this brought them a little closer. When they landed, they had still had two hours to spare. The city greeted them under a mantle of fog and a tacky, light drizzle that stuck to the skin. The museum was near the company they had to visit and they read on the door that admission was free. She suggested they go in. He thought it was a good way to kill time. Now he wasn't so sure. With the business of the meeting taken care of, he didn't know what else to talk about. His companion looked absorbed, or apathetic. When they finished the avian section and turned into the hall with the mammals, she stopped abruptly with a brief—and nervous, he thought—burst of laughter.

"Mustelids!"

"What?"

"Mustelids."

"Mustelids?"

"I've always liked them. They're my favorite animals."

He repeated her words slowly, looking at her cautiously.

"You like them. They're your favorites."

"Otters, in particular. Sea otters. You know what they look like? Have you seen their faces? They're so expressive . . ."

"Otters."

"And the name. The name itself: *mustelids*. It's kind of amusing, right? It sounds nice. Words with three syllables usually do."

He shook his head.

"You're surprising, sometimes."

Why? She grew serious. What was strange about liking them? Mustelids—with their long bodies and short legs—are small animals with a great deal of nuance, she explained. They're invaders and destroyers, and they can do so much damage to fields that in small towns they're hated, hunted, caught with traps and beaten with sticks. Aggressive, but wary, too, they seek shelter in their lairs, which they only leave at night to cause trouble or get run over on some secondary highway. And they're tenacious, natural born survivors: there are subspecies spread throughout the world. They adapt easily to all environments since they'll eat anything, or almost anything. Sure, they're cute, but not if you try to pet them: their little teeth will break the skin in a second, not so damn cute then. Most people don't really like them, they're disgusted, repulsed by them, like by rodents. But teenagers love ferrets. They walk them on leashes and sometimes even get them to fight for fun. And mink and sable fur certainly appeal to some, don't they?

"Aren't you the expert . . . I didn't even know that otters belonged to the same family as . . ." he hesitated, ". . . ferrets and weasels."

Her eyes flashed. "Of course they're from the same family. It's just that otters have a more good-natured, roly-poly look."

He took note of the words she used—"good-natured," "roly-poly"—and thought how few people talked like that nowadays. Actually, she was speaking in a way that she hadn't spoken on the plane, with more emphasis and less apathy, though she was still very serious—a childish seriousness, even. She asked him if he had seen the video of the two sea otters that slept holding hands, floating on their backs. No, he said. No? He really hadn't seen it? It was so funny. The video had gone viral; everyone had talked about it and linked to it. Someone put relaxing music in the background to emphasize the peacefulness of the scene and . . .

"Was it filmed in a zoo?" he interrupted.

"What?"

"Were the otters in captivity? Who took the video?"

What does it matter, she said. She frowned. It might have been in a zoo. There were voices in the background, people laughing, kids, so it must not have been in the wild. What does it matter, she repeated. She approached a glass case to observe a stuffed badger. It was a large specimen, as big as a medium-sized dog. Its tiny glass eyes, set close together, gave it a hostile look.

"A friend told me that they sell cartons of badger urine. A liter of badger urine, can you imagine? Going to the store to buy that. I think they use it for hunting. They soak the base of trees with urine and the dogs go crazy, it gets them ready to run and be on alert and detect prey."

He also looked at the badger's striped face, feigning interest.

"I've never heard that. Badger urine," he repeated. "My grandmother used to say that badger butter was good for asthma. My father had asthma, and I . . . I have it, too. She—my grandmother—always went on about the butter, but I never knew if it was just an old wives' tale or if it really worked. What is badger butter, anyway? I mean, where do you get it? Do they sell it, or what? How do you use it? Do you rub it all over your chest, do you . . . spread it on toast and eat it?"

He laughed and scratched his head. His joke hadn't worked. He changed his tone.

"Asthma is awful. The feeling of suffocation is pure agony. You only understand if you've been through it. When I have an asthma attack, there's nothing I can do. And all that about the badger butter and my grandmother, well, it's just dumb because . . . I never did get to try it."

He stopped speaking. She had stopped listening a while before. She was a few feet ahead, hunched in front of a case of smaller animals: weasels, ermines, minks, and martens, all immortalized in surveillance or attack positions, as if they were following a group strategy. She read the signs very carefully, inspecting them to confirm that the details in the descriptions were correct. Crouched, her coat dragging on the floor, she explained that an ermine's fur changed according to the season, although the tip of the tail was always, *always* black. As if she hadn't just read that, he thought. He couldn't understand her enthusiasm. They were ugly and unlikeable animals, in his opinion. Maybe they had their charm when they were alive, but the stuffed ones were actually very unpleasant. He imagined their cries would be piercing and hysteric. Two of them—two weasels?—were set opposite each other and gave the ridiculous impression that they were chatting or arguing. He said they reminded him of a Walter Potter piece. She didn't answer. Was she familiar with Walter Potter? Was it worth explaining it to her? Then he remembered something even better to get her attention; he smiled to himself before calling her by name. "Nuria," he said. She turned with a contrary gesture, as if he had touched her, and looked at him, expectant.

"You know the painting by Da Vinci, *Lady with an Ermine*? Did you know that there wasn't any ermine in the first version?"

That was the kind of fact that he usually tucked away in

his brain when he read the Sunday newspaper supplements. Dates and locations of the best Walter Potter exhibits. The story of *Lady with an Ermine*. Da Vinci's birthday. Date of his death. The girl responded, slightly offended.

"Of course I know that painting. Everyone knows it. How do they know that about the ermine? Did they do one of those scientific studies that take years and cost a fortune? Just to know whether or not a few brushstrokes were really Da Vinci's?"

"They were all Da Vinci's, but he painted it in several phases. When they analyzed the paint, they discovered that originally it had been a much more conventional portrait. It was common during that period to paint ladies' mysterious glances, watching as their lovers came through a door. But the analysis also showed that the painting had been retouched, and that the first version of the ermine was smaller, more delicate than the one we know. Supposedly the animal represented a duke, and the lady was a favored mistress. And this duke wasn't at all convinced by how it turned out, so he asked Da Vinci to go back and paint a bigger, stronger ermine, because the first one wasn't . . . befitting of his station. So, in the third version, the animal is muscular, robust . . . with a lot of presence in the painting."

"So, Da Vinci did what they asked?"

"Of course. He painted portraits according to what the subjects wanted. What was he going to do? Refuse?"

"No, no, that part's fine. I don't care about that. What interests me is that the woman is holding an ermine. A creature like that wouldn't let itself be held so easily. I mean, if it wasn't real, if it was supposed to symbolize something else, not just a pet, Da Vinci could have painted a lion or a tiger or whatever. Something fiercer to make the duke happy, something more . . . virile. When you make things into symbols, you can do what you want with them, right?"

He focused on her smile. Was she being ironic? When she mentioned symbols, was she referring to her stories? He still hadn't finished reading them. He'd had the book for a few months, but had only read the first three. He hadn't liked them. He didn't know why, but they gave him an uneasy feeling. Maybe he had expected something sweeter, or simpler. But those stories, the subtle ambiguity, the dark insinuations . . . they were too disturbing. Since reading them he had looked at her with more curiosity. A woman who writes in her free time and had even gotten her book published, but who doesn't go announcing it all over the place—he'd found out by chance and bought the book without saying anything—all of that appealed to him. It gave her an aura of intelligence; intelligence, depth, and culture, he thought, that's why he was so struck to see her almost stretched out on the floor, pointing at a stone marten. How could this be the same person? The same person who explained—as if he actually cared!—the differences between marten pelts. Stone martens and pine martens: he was as uninterested in them as she probably had been in his Da Vinci story, but at least he tried to pretend. And what was it that interested her? Did she really like those horrible stuffed creatures? Because they worked as symbols? Were there symbols in her stories? Symbols he hadn't grasped? What was she trying to say in them, exactly? He had felt that something escaped him as he read, suspecting that something wasn't clear, or defined, or even intentional. Or maybe she simply played with misinterpretation as embellishment, to make herself look important. Like painting a bigger ermine where at first there had only been blank space, he thought.

He was irritated.

She crossed the hall from one case to another, pressing her hands against the glass, leaving handprints, smiling to herself. She wasn't much better than the kids with the dinosaurs, he thought, and then remembered another interesting fact. He approached her from behind. He wanted to put his hand on her shoulder, say her name again—*Nuria*—but he held back. He simply spoke, overcoming the fear of sounding pedantic or annoying.

"NASA used to use ferrets to lay cables in their buildings. I saw it in a documentary once. Their bodies are so flexible that they can go through extremely narrow holes and slip into tiny spaces. They didn't have any other way, so they used ferrets. And they used them for Princess Diana and Prince Charles's wedding, too. Of course that was a long time ago, we were just kids, but I heard the television and sound cables were installed using ferrets. There was a big to-do because one escaped and they didn't know where it had gone. They looked everywhere but couldn't find it and they had to start the ceremony. It turned up later in the back row. Imagine what a scene that was, all of a sudden a ferret under the ladies' skirts, guests screaming, up on the pews."

They laughed. He liked her laugh. He felt satisfied that he'd finally gotten it out of her. Satisfied and victorious, but the resentment was still there, even if he couldn't determine its exact origins. They had reached the end of the hall, where several otters were displayed—river and marine, large and small, brown and black. Silently, they read the sign that underscored the otter's high degree of intelligence: *An otter will take a stone from the bottom of the sea and, lying on its back, place the stone on its chest and hit mussels against it until they crack open. With the exception of primates, otters are the only mammals capable of using a tool in this way.* She turned and looked at him smugly. See? she said. What was he supposed to see? Did she find that fact so very incredible? Was this a reason to sign up for the Intelligent Otter Fan Club? How was any of that important? He realized that communication between their two worlds was impossible. They were together, yes, on the same job, in the same city, on the same mission, and now in the same museum, but maybe that was all they shared: the setting.

On the way to the museum café, the girl wanted to stop in the gift shop.

"The kids don't bother you anymore?"

She didn't answer. She lingered over the stuffed animals, the coloring books, the plastic figurines. She bought a little albino otter, for a price he found absurd.

"It's very well-made," she explained. "I collect these figurines."

This time, it was he who didn't answer.


As they waited for their coffee, she turned the toy over in her hands without looking at it. He broke the silence. His voice sounded uneven and hoarse. He froze up a little, but then spoke with all the strength he could muster.

"You know, I bought your book. I've read your stories."

She reddened. She nodded slightly, as if to thank him, but didn't say a word. He didn't know what to do next. Did he have to tell her that he had liked them? Pretend that he had read the whole thing? Ask her why she never talked about them, about her stories? What did she expect him to say? What was she used to getting from her readers? Admiration, respect, questions, criticism? Before continuing, he briefly studied her fingers. She bit her nails, or at least she didn't take very good care of them. She was still twisting the little otter in her hands, tapping it nervously with her index finger. Maybe she was waiting. He felt forced to go on without knowing what he was saying.

"But it seems contradictory. If someone read your stories without knowing you, well, without knowing anything about you, I guess they'd find something coherent in them, some meaning—" he stressed the word *meaning*. "But seeing you, the way you are, the way you talk, your way of being in the world, I don't know . . . there's something that doesn't make sense in your writing, something that doesn't fit."

She halted the movement of her fingers. She looked at him with interest. Her eyes wavered slightly. He realized that his words had destabilized her, and now he couldn't stop.

"There's no way that you like otters because they're . . . amusing . . . that's the word you used, right? *Amusing* . . . because they hold hands while they nap and you saw it in a 'funny' video . . . or because you turn into a whimsical kid when you go into a gift shop and you buy yourself *that*," he pointed derisively at the figurine, "and then you write, I don't know, horrible stories about suicide and depression and incest."

She cleared her throat and asked him to go on. And he did, furious.

"And your characters, so dark, so . . . shady? They're always bitter, or sad, or straight up selfish and evil. They have no compassion, no remorse. Why do they have to be like that? Are those the kinds of people you come in contact with? That you live with every day? Is everyone like that?"

There was a brief silence. His last words echoed between them. *Is everyone like that?* She made a wry face. He had the impression that she was concentrating on coming up with a valid answer. But she didn't speak. She looked up and then, with effort, said: "Actually . . ."

Just the one word, *actually*, and then she stopped, on guard, when the waitress set their drinks down on the table. He didn't think the waitress's interruption was a good enough reason to stop talking, but she didn't go on. She grabbed a small packet of sugar, tore it open slowly, and didn't say anything else.

"What? *Actually* what? What do you *actually* think? You're not going to finish?"

The girl shrugged. Who cared? He lost his patience.

"No. You can't just say that nothing matters. Every time I ask you why something is the way it is and not another way, you say the same thing: who cares. Do you think I'm not capable of understanding? That it's not even worth making the effort? Or is it that you don't have an answer?"

His eyes were wet, not hers. She limited herself to looking at him without blinking. She opened and closed her mouth a few times without articulating a single word. Their coffees grew cold. A pair of teachers who had been circling to see if they were leaving their table approached them, their credentials pinned on their shirts. She looked up and waved her hand dismissively. No, she said, they weren't going yet, and on making that gesture it was like she came out from under a spell, a kind of hypnosis, because her faced changed, something undefined but perceptible changed in her and she looked at him differently.

She didn't have to explain herself to him, she said, but then she told him about the tightrope. The tightrope, she insisted. She told him that she felt like she was walking on one—on a tightrope—all the time. She emphasized the words *all the time*. She constantly felt like she could fall, she said, that she could slip off one side or the other and fall into the abyss. Not even the possibility of moving forward gave her the slightest sense of stability because at the end of the rope, at the end of all the effort, she knew there was nothing. He blinked in astonishment.

"See, you're talking in innuendos again, like it's us—and not you—who have to find the meaning."

But he was becoming more relaxed, his anger was dissolving. He wanted her to keep talking, to explain that the significance wasn't hidden, that it wasn't about making connections or having to interpret anything. She was talking about a tightrope and that was it, as if there were a real rope, a tightrope as real or as fake as those mounted animals or the plastic toys in the gift shop. He listened to her carefully, almost emotionally. She told him that she often found herself on the edge of tears. She could start to cry at any moment, as soon as someone or something touched her. She wasn't talking about physical touch, although that, too, and he remembered when he had said her name and how she had started. Her body was full of buttons to be pressed, she explained, some led to laughter and others to tears, sometimes they led to both at once, but she never knew how she would react beforehand.

"I live without preconceptions, in other words."

He thought he understood her. He knew she was speaking to him as sincerely—or with as little artifice—as she was able to. He wanted to stand up and hug her, to hold her close to him, though he knew he could never do that, and moreover, he knew he wouldn't have in any case. But hold her hand? Yes, maybe. First, he stretched out his arm in her direction, and then his fingers. He didn't even get close enough to brush his hand against hers. He just grabbed the little otter that she had dropped, instinctively, when she saw him come close.

"You need this to escape, right?"

The toy? She raised her eyebrows. No, she said, it wasn't an escape. The otters, ferrets, martens—stuffed or not—weren't an escape. That was just her, she said. She repeated it to herself: *That's me.* The escape was just the opposite: writing as a way out. She summoned danger by writing about it, and in giving form to horror, she prevented its realization. She escaped. Was it unnecessary, pointless? Fine, well then she'll apologize.

"Seriously, I apologize."

But she didn't know to whom.


She fell asleep on his shoulder on the return flight. The meeting had gone as planned; none of those present— including the heads of the company—had gone off the script that they had predicted with such professionalism. One could say it had been a success. Nevertheless, they were worn out, exhausted. The lunch post-meeting had been long and boring. They had checked their watches furtively. They all had, the visitors and the visited alike. The conversation had more than run its course when the time to leave finally came. He was relieved, ready to resume their hard-won intimacy, but he realized on the way to the airport that she wasn't relaxing. She was as reserved as she had been in the meeting, her lips pressed together, an impenetrable look on her face, as though the conversation in the museum café had never existed. Even the visit to the museum itself—the entrance clogged with children, the stuffed specimens in their glass cases, the gift shop—seemed unreal. He had waited for that moment—to be alone with her again—to keep talking about tightropes and mustelids, but when he saw that he'd have to start over from the beginning, instead of being discouraged, he was overcome with animosity. She was a fraud, he thought now, as he felt her uneven breathing, the slight movements of her head when the plane shook with turbulence or she trembled in a dream. Or maybe she was faking, he thought, maybe she was pretending to be asleep to avoid talking to him, or maybe she just wanted the chance to touch him—her cheek on his shoulder—without her pride or her good name—that of the evasive, distant girl, so hard to approach—being affected in the least. A prude, after she'd written all that stuff about masturbation and the scene with the dog and everything else that he hadn't read yet but knew was there, locked in the pages of her book: stories she'd put there to hurt and disturb him and countless others, handing off her bundle of misery to those who weren't guilty of anything. She slept practically the whole flight and only at the end, when the pilot announced the landing, did she open her eyes, blink a few times, remember where she was, and separate herself from him brusquely, apologizing again.

"I must have been bothering you the whole flight."

She played the innocent, she was clearly playing the innocent, he said to himself, and he watched her from the corner of his eye, how she gathered her bag from the floor, how she redid her ponytail: when she raised her arms to her hair he was vaguely aroused, and this made him even angrier. He watched her turn and look out the window—even though it was so cloudy you couldn't see a thing—and then, as he watched her put on her coat, he saw the albino otter slip from her pocket and fall into the crack between the seats, hidden there, without her realizing. Then they landed, waited as long as they had to—minutes, in silence—and filed out in the cramped line, following the couple with the baby whose wailing hadn't woken her in all that time, more proof—he thought—that she had feigned being asleep.

It wasn't until they had exited the aircraft and were on the little staircase leading to the runway that she put her hands in her pockets and noted the absence of the figurine. She gave another one of her exaggerated starts and turned back to look for it inside the cabin, as if rescuing that meaningless toy was a matter of life and death, not caring in the least about the commotion, the delay, the inconvenience she caused the other passengers who were coming down as she went back up. Nor did she care about his embarrassment, as he stood in the middle of the stairs, unsure of whether to keep going or wait for her there, like an absolute idiot.

**SARA MESA** is the author of eight works of fiction, including *Scar* (winner of the Ojo Critico Prize), *Four by Four* (a finalist for the Herralde Prize), *An Invisible Fire* (winner of the Premio Málaga de Novela), and *Among the Hedges*. Her works have been translated into more than ten different languages, and have been widely praised for their concise, sharp style.

**KATIE WHITTEMORE** is a graduate of the University of New Hampshire (BA), Cambridge University (M.Phil), and Middlebury College (MA), and was a 2018 Bread Loaf Translators Conference participant. Her work has appeared or is forthcoming in *Two Lines*, *The Arkansas International*, *The Common Online*, *Gulf Coast Magazine Online*, *The Los Angeles Review*, *The Brooklyn Rail*, and *In Translation*. Current projects include novels by Spanish authors Javier Serena, Aliocha Coll, Aroa Moreno Durán, Nuria Labari, Katixa Agirre, and Juan Gómez Bárcena.

**OPEN
LETTER**

**WWW.OPENLETTERBOOKS.ORG**

**OPEN LETTER**

**OPEN
LETTER**